WHERE THE OLD PEOPLE PLAY

Harold Alexander Jr.

About the Author

Harold Alexander Jr. grew up in Houston, Texas. After graduating from college, he moved to a small town in southwestern Louisiana where he now resides, along with his wife and sons. He has devoted his entire life to working with underprivileged and troubled youth. He is also a minister of the Gospel. In his spare time he enjoys reading, traveling, and collecting coins. Above all, he relishes in the priceless advice obtained from elderly people.

Acknowledgements

The writing of this book was a tedious process, and my typing skills are nearly nonexistent. As I was handwriting this book, my wife, Angela, would take my manuscript and start typing. She seemed to love doing this. Angela encouraged me during the writing process, saying how great she thought the characters were. She also worked endlessly to find a publisher and took the helm making publishing decisions. Her technical assistance was priceless. I could not have achieved my dream of being a published author without the loving, dedicated support, and persistence of Angela. Thank you my love. You are my best friend.

I would also like to honor my mother and siblings. There are not enough words in the English vocabulary to express how much my mom has meant to me. I am the man I am today because of her. She shows me through everything she does what love is. She gave me the words in which to express how I feel. Thank you for giving me words.

To my siblings, Mark, Troy, Kimberly, Terrance, and Torian, thank you all for being my early childhood friends in those rainy days. My childhood was fantastic because of you. You always allowed me to be me.

To my daughter, Sacha, my sons, Gus, Bryce, Timothy, and Harold III, and my grandchildren, Gianni and Cameron, you have filled my life with immeasurable joy.

Most of all, I want to acknowledge two of the most magnificent women the Lord has ever made- my grandmothers, Louella Alexander, and Anna Bell Davenport, who have nurtured and guided me along life's way, and to my dear father-in-law, Jefferson 'Normie' Johnson Jr, who always enjoy playing where the old people play.

Dedication

This book is dedicated to my father, Harold Alexander Sr., who inspired me with his words, and without truly knowing, gave me a love for reading. He often thought as children, I, and my other siblings, watched too much television. One day he said "Turn that television off and go read a book." These words became an often repeated sermon of my father and still ring true in my ears today. I even preach this sermon to my own kids. He never suggested what to read; just to read. Thank you, Dad, because it was through reading I wanted to write. I love you with all my heart.

Your son, your firstborn,

Harold Jr.

ILLUSTRATIONS BY:

GUS GRANGER JR.

TABLE OF CONTENTS

INTRODUCTION

I watch them, but they can't see me. A biscuit, black coffee, and conversation is what they order. This place is familiar to them, and everybody knows each other's names; everybody but me. But they can't see me. They nod and smile and even say hello, affirming my presence, but they can't see me. I've noticed that they sit in the same seats every day as if their names are imprinted there, but they can't see me. As always, the aroma of expensive perfume catches my sense of smell as I pass them. But they can't see me. How dare I invade their space? How dare I involve myself in their conversation or even ask, "What's the name of that fine perfume you're wearing?" because they can't see me.

I don't know their names, but I've given them names. One woman has red hair. She wears red-rimmed glasses that match her perfectly styled hair. I call her Ms. Red. Another woman has gray hair with a blue tint. Her dresses and jewelry are of exceptional quality. I call her the Elegant Lady. She looks like she is the oldest woman in the group. One man has a hat that has a World War II emblem on it. I wonder what he has seen, how it has affected him. I want to ask, but I dare not because he can't see me. I call him the Vet. There's another man who uses a cane. I wonder what has brought him to need the assistance of a cane. Was he injured at any time in his life, or is it just a natural progression of where he now plays? I call him the Courageous Gentleman. There's another lady with gray hair. She seems like the youngest in the group. She doesn't talk much, but I can tell she's listening. I call her the Quiet Lady. There's another man who wears a lot of all-in-one jumpsuits. He seems to be the oldest of them all. He is the one who plays the hardest in the group. He is very jolly, making sure everybody is having a good time where the old people play. He is able to bring humor to their most hurtful and serious moments of life shared on this playground. I call him Mr. Jolly. I have names for them all, but they can't see me.

They all look different, but there's something familiar about their faces. The lines. The wrinkles. The creases. Each line, each wrinkle, each crease tells a story. And I listen. And boy, do I listen! But they can't see me. What would they say if they knew I was invading their space? What would they say if they knew I was listening to some of their most intimate moments? Would they invite me in to play? Or would they tell me to come back in a few years when I'm older? One thing I do know—they could never play in my playground again. But if I live long enough, I will play in theirs. So, I listen. Oh boy, do I listen! And still, they can't see me.

Sometimes when I listen I feel like crying. I want to cry because some of the stories are so sad. And I feel like crying because some of the stories are so happy and touching. And even though I hear them speak of tragedy, I never hear them complain. But I don't cry because my sons who are with me will ask, "Daddy, why are you crying?" And then my boys will know that I've been listening. Oh boy, have I been listening! They share a language that seems to be just their language, yet I understand what they are saying. Like butterflies drawn to the flames of a fire, like bugs drawn to the street lights at night, they draw me in, but they can't see me. As they talk, I can tell they have probably forgotten more than I know, so I listen, and boy, do I listen.

They are not much older than me, yet I know they are more experienced. The youngest is maybe a generation away, and when they speak, it is not from what they have heard but from a deeper conviction of trial and error, from self-exploration—they know.

Chapter One
MS. RED

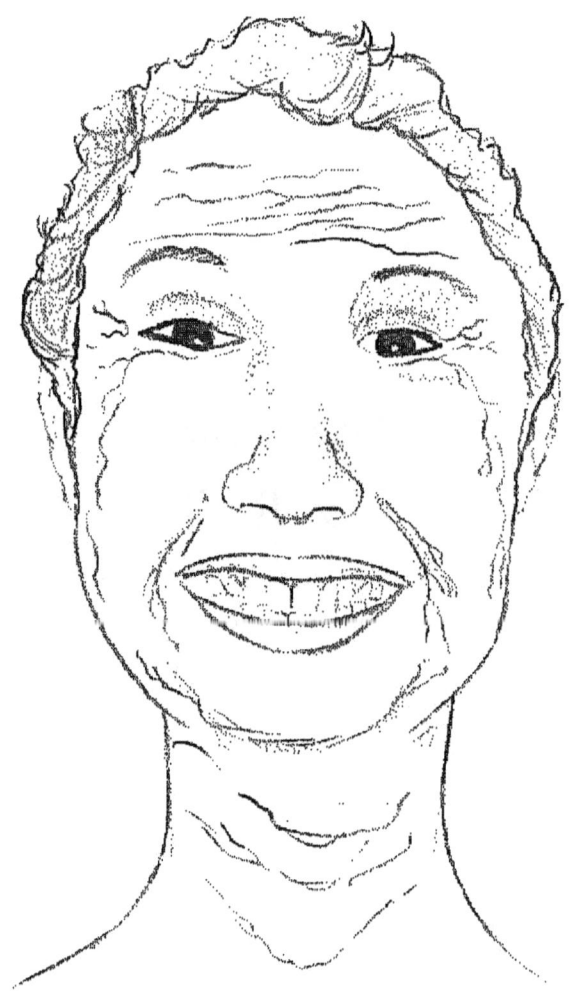

Ms. Red always seems to initiate the conservations as she speaks of her youth, of being young again. I watch as the corners of her mouth turn upward to form a smile, and there is a sparkle in her eyes that tell me, as she talks of her youth, that she is revisiting a good place, a very good place. My ear leans in their direction, trying to absorb as much as I can of the words of gold that will soon flow from her mouth. I think I hear her say she was a dancer, a ballerina, and although Father Time and Mother Nature have visited her, in my mind's eye, I can see the ballerina in her. Maybe it's her posture and the nape of her neck. Maybe it's her still-defined calf muscle or the gestures she makes with her arms and hands or the pirouettes she bravely performs right there in our presence, on their playground, that serve as proof of the truths she tells.

And right there at that moment (like the little boy who is too young to go outside to play as he looks out the window of his house and watches the other kids play), I want to play with them, but I don't belong on their playground. She says she wanted her daughter to be a ballerina, but she chose another path, yet she loves her daughter deeply and is proud of the woman she has become. She reaches into her purse to take out a picture; it's a picture of her teen granddaughter dressed in a tutu and ballerina shoes. A daughter's divorce has brought these three generations of ladies under the same roof, and it's her daughter's daughter who will be the constant, beautiful, joyful tears reminder of her youthful days of dance, the rehearsals, the long hours of strenuous practices, the performances, the camera flashes, the standing ovations, and she smiles—oh boy, what a smile!

Again she speaks of youth but not her youth, just youth—wasted youth, the recklessness, restlessness, and the ungratefulness that is lacking from some of the young people of today. And she wonders what kind of world it will be for her granddaughter. She adores her granddaughter, but she worries. Is this worry the cause of the deep creases in her face? This tells me that she has been playing here for some time. I listen closer as she talks of a time when phrases like "Yes sir," "No, ma'am," "Thank you," "Pretty please," and "May I?" were common practices taught to kids by their parents. She speaks of times past, when fathers taught their sons how to shake another man's hand, tie neckties, and change a flat tire on a car. During those times, mothers taught their daughters how to curtsy and bow before they danced and how to cook a meal. Gentlemen found opening doors for women commonplace. They also tipped their hats in the presence of a lady. A gentlemen caller came to the door and knocked, and parents had the chance to watch him sweat as the father asked him what seemed to be a million questions. Who are your parents? What does your father do? Where are you taking my daughter? What time are you going to be back, and will there be adult chaperones? By the way, he is about to take dad's little angel out on a date.

And for a moment, I am transported back in time. I can feel her words, I can touch her words, I can see her words, but they can't see me. She speaks of a time not too far away from my own yet far away enough from me to only wish I could have played there, back when. Back when a handshake meant something, back when chivalry was alive and real, back when a man would pull out the chair for a woman to sit before he would sit. Back when every neighbor knew his neighbor, back when children were children, girls were girly, and men were manly, back when every man pulled his own weight. Back when family took care of family. Back when a man took pride in his work, and he worked hard.

Ms. Red speaks and shares of her past, it seems as if, for a moment, time stands still, and the whole world has paused. And we have been given a glimpse of a time passed, a page of history that will never happen again; so, I cry, but they can't see me. And as if I could not be drawn in any more than I already am, I pull my chair closer, and I wonder, can they see me now? But I guess not, for Ms. Red continues speaking as if not to notice me at all. And as she speaks, she only pauses to welcome the comments of the others who play on this playground.

And as always, Mr. Jolly can't believe Ms. Red was once a ballet dancer. As if she has not been truthful in her speech, he asks her to perform another pirouette that she gladly performs. His response to her performance is to say, "I believed you the first time. I just wanted to see you do it again," which caused the whole group to break out in laughter.

Totally unaware of her surroundings, Ms. Red's pirouette has drawn an audience that fondly claps as she once again takes her seat. How many times has she heard the cheers and the applause of an audience? How many times has she received the accolades from a crowd for an award-winning performance? How many encores has she answered in her days of twirling, high jumps, high lifts, toe raises, and elegantly per-formed moves? And even now, she still seeks the cheers, the applause, the accolades, and the encore of the crowd. With this small audience, she rises from her seat to acknowledge their acceptance of her small performance, and she curtsies and bows and quietly says, "Thank you."

She sits again and softly and quietly continues speaking to the other old folks on the playground, but this time, the mood and tone have changed. An air of sadness has filled the playground. I am too far away to hear her words yet too close not to get caught up in this sadness. What did she say to change the atmosphere so fast? I can say coming from the South, we have grown accustomed to fast weather changes. I can recall the many mornings of sunshine and heat only to be replaced in a matter of hours with cold temperatures and rain.

I inch closer, and I hear her say, "He has been dead for forty-five years." From her tears, I gather it was either a husband or a son, and from her next words spoken, it gets clarified. She says, "He was and is the love of my life." I had wondered at one time of her speaking was she married, was she divorced, had she ever been married, had he died; now

5

all my questions about this intimate part of her life would be answered, and so I listen. Boy, do I listen!

She speaks of the day they first met, and she speaks with such vivid details that it brings all of us to that day. She was a teenage girl about the same age as her granddaughter. The local butcher shop delivery boy stopped in to her ballet class that was held in the old local department store to warm himself while he was on his way to make his last delivery. This old local department store had recently been renovated to become the new ballet school.

When he walked in, he had interrupted their class. The instructor, whose back was toward the door, was at first unaware of his presence but became aware of his presence when it was obvious by the reaction of the non-practicing, whispering, giggly girls that they found this intruder to be extremely handsome. As the instructor turned around to see who had caused these young ladies to pause in their practice and had them in such a frenzy, she politely asked, "May I help you, young man?" He kindly answered "I apologize, ma'am; I did not mean to interrupt your class, but I am on my way to my last delivery, and as you can see, it is really cold outside, and this place was the only one still open where I could come in for a bit to warm myself before I continue on my journey. I'll just stand here by the door, if you don't mind, and I promise I won't interrupt your class again." The instructor clapped her hands and said, "Now girls, let's get back to work, and let this young man warm himself before he continues on his journey."

While at first he had caught their attention, these young ladies had now caught his attention. He stood by the door and turned around to see them elegantly perform twirls, pirouettes, spins, toe raises, hand gestures, and other ballet moves. And as he watched, he had gotten so caught up in it that now he had become part of them as he tried to perform the same, exact moves. After a long day of chopping, freezing, and wrapping meat in paper bags for delivery, watching these girls had put a smile on his face and a song in his heart, and it was a pleasant distraction from all that meat. And there was one red-haired, pony-tailed, long-legged girl who, while she danced, had put a twinkle in his eye.

He then tried to perform a pirouette that caused him to hit his butt on the floor. The feminine giggly messes of estrogen immediately paused and laughed as they now watched their uninvited visitor make a fool out of himself. As he raised himself from the floor, he once again apologized to the instructor. "Ma'am, I'm sorry for disrupting your class again. I guess it is time for me to get going. Thank you, I really enjoyed seeing the girls dance." As he began pushing open the door to leave, he turned and asked, "Ma'am, would it be all right if from time to time I stop in to see the girls dance?" After hearing the answer, he smiled and quickly ran out the door. But there was another one smiling about the news she had just heard—she would see him again.

Weeks passed, and there was no sign of the boy who came in from the cold. The season changed, and still no sign. Every day she would look toward the door, her heart hoping that today would be that day, but no sign.

And then, just when her heart had stopped hoping, he walked in. But there were no bags in his hands and no deliveries to be made. And he had an unusual request of the instructor. He asked if he could join their class. The teacher's mouth dropped.

In this town, boys played sports, drove tractors, rode horses, and chopped down trees. This town was a man's town, but the boy who came in from the cold was no ordinary boy. He was not afraid in this time of conformity to be independent. He was not afraid to step out from the norm and be an individual. He was not afraid to dare to be different. Was his newfound love of dance the reason he wanted to join the class, or was his real reason for joining this class a plan to get closer to the red-haired, pony-tailed, long-legged girl who had put a twinkle in his eye?

He knew he would be the talk of this small town. He knew his male friends would make him the butt of many jokes. The men of the town would ask his father what was wrong with his son. Yet, in spite of what he knew, he still dared to be different, and even if the real reason was to get close to Red, it later came to show her how much he was willing to do and how far he was willing to go to be close to her. By the way, he wasn't a very good dancer.

Her story has us sitting on the edge of our seats wanting more, begging for more, yearning for more, so we asked her to continue. How dare I say "we" and "us!" How dare I invade their playground? How dare I continue to listen to their life stories? I feel a twinge of guilt, yet in spite of myself, I can't help it. So, I continue to listen, even though I really can't say anything, for they can't see me.

After this day, when he walked back into the class, he and Red would never be apart again. He joined their class in spite of the town's laughter; a boy, a country boy, practicing ballet. He exchanged his overalls for tights, he exchanged his cowboy boots for ballet shoes, and the rate of exchange was outstanding! He got the chance to be close to Red.

Because of the smallness of this town, after ballet practice, the girls walked home in a group. I guess girls have always been groupish. This walking group not only offered friendship but also provided safety. They all lived next door to one another.

On this day, the boy asked if he could walk them home, yet they all knew who he really wanted to walk home, and this practice became the norm. The boy lived in the more rural part of town, so after seeing Red home, he would get on his delivery bike. He walked the bike as he walked with the girls, and then he rode the rest of the way home. He lived three miles outside of town, and on this three-mile ride, all he thought about was Red. He wondered, did she ever think about him? This practice went on for months—the walk, the ride, the walk, the ride, the walk, the ride; it was now time for him to find out her feelings toward him. Everybody knew how he felt about her. He just wanted to ask her how she felt about him, which was the direct approach, but he wasn't that bold. What if she did not feel the same way he did? Could he take that rejection?

So, he decided to ask her for a date. "Would you care to go out with me this Saturday to the movies?" His knees buckled, and he smiled as he received a "yes." On this day, he a made it home in record time and shared the news with his family. His father told him that the proper thing to do now would be to go to her house and ask her father if he could take his daughter out on a date. He asked her on a Monday, and the date was scheduled for Saturday. Saturday was his first day off during the week, and there was no ballet rehearsal. That night, he did not sleep at all. Tuesday was waiting for him. This was the day that after seeing her home from practice, instead of riding away, he would have to meet her father and ask him if he could date his daughter. At school, he was a nervous wreck and kept rehearsing what he would say to her father, moving his lips, whispering words, and sweating. All his classmates thought something was terribly wrong with him. And if he was already sweating, just imagine what he would do at the official introduction to ask about the date.

Ms. Red paused, and we paused for a moment to look around, since everybody on the playground was quiet. Ms. Red had taken us on an emotional roller coaster ride. We had laughed a lot, we had signed often, and we had *oohed* and *aahed*. We had smiled because she had drawn us into her world, her past, and we loved it. She continued, and our eyes and ears begged for more.

It was now Tuesday after deliveries and rehearsal. He walked his bike and the girls home; the girls had been giggling all the way home, for they knew what was about to occur: one in their group of estrogen was about to go on her first date. At rehearsal, Red had told her group of twirling, twisting, turning, leaping, ballet training friends every little detail of her soon-to-be first date.

The boy was still nervous, and he was only moments away, a few feet away from his destination. He was a little more confident than before. I forgot to tell you that Monday night, his older brother, who was a student of the local small college, had given him a few pointers on how to approach the "Sweat Causer." I mean, Red's father! He says, first knock on the door, and ask to speak to the man of the house. "May I speak to the man of the house, please?" When and if they ask you to come in, stand near the door, and wait for their instruction. Someone may ask you to come in and take a seat. When the father enters the room, stand up, look him straight in the eyes, give him a firm handshake, and introduce yourself. He will already know your name, but this is just a formality and official introduction.

The father already knew everything about the boy—the ballet boy, the delivery boy, the boy who had been walking his daughter home. Just make a good first impression, and you got it made in the shade. That's how they talked back then. His brother continued to tell him that while still looking her father in the eyes, ask him if you could take his daughter to the movies. The boy was also glad that his own father had spent nearly a whole day in the past showing him how to shake another man's hand.

He knocked on the door, and her mom opened the door. Red went in. The boy proceeded, "May I speak to the man of the house, please?" he asked with a smile. Mother said, "Yes, I will get him for you. Come on in and take a seat." The house was a beautiful place, beautifully decorated with pictures and sports trophies and ballet awards everywhere. Red was an exceptional dancer, as was her mother, evidenced by some of the older pictures and trophies.

When her dad entered the room, the boy rose from his seat, extended his hand, looked him in his eyes, and said, "Good evening, Red's father. I am Jones Williamson, Jr. My parents are Mr. and Ms. Jones Williamson, Sr., and, for months, I have walked your daughter and the other girls back home from ballet practice. And I guess you already know why I am here, as I am sure that your daughter has conveyed to you the purpose of my visit. I am here to ask you, sir, with your permission, to take your daughter on a date to the movies." He continued. "My mother will come by and pick up your daughter around five thirty to drop us to the six o'clock movies. My younger brother and maybe your younger daughter can come along, too. Then my mother will come to pick us up from the movies and bring us to the soda shop. I will make sure that your daughter is safely home by nine."

Dad was impressed. He was more than impressed. He had been watching this boy even before the boy had been watching his daughter. He admired the boy, as he had observed him making his deliveries and had even noticed how he approached his delivery job with a smile and plenty of energy. He noticed how he always reported to work on time, and he even knew that the talk around town was that a boy joined ballet classes to be close to his daughter. Respecting the way the boy stood up, firmly shaking his hand and looking him straight in the eyes, her father said, "Son, I know who you are, and I also know your parents, and you have shown me and told me everything I need to know. And, yes, you can take my daughter on her first date."

While the boy and father were talking, Red and her mother had excused themselves to the next room but had their ears pressed to the door so they could hear every single word. As the boy stood up to leave, he shook her father's hand again, a little firmer than before, affirming with the handshake and the big smile on his face his great joy of hearing the word "yes" and said, "Thank you, sir, and would you please tell the misses and Red goodnight for me?" He rode his bike home as quickly as he could. He ran through the door and told his family, who had been waiting for his arrival, the good news. Now he really had gotten nervous.

He thought he had made a good impression with Red's father. He now wondered how he could impress Red. He would soon learn that it's the small things that impress a woman who is in love. It is opening doors; it is listening to her as she talks; it is when you reach to hold her hand just because; it is complementing the fine meal she just cooked; it is noticing the new dress she just bought that fits her body well, accentuating all the physical assets you like about her; it is noticing her new hairdo; and it is liking the new perfume she is wearing. It is still dating her after many years of being married. It is the smile that crosses your face when she walks into the room, and yes, it is even sharing the not-so-good times that make this first date the one you always remember. It is saying, "I'm sorry," when you've done something wrong; it is saying, "Thank you," so she won't feel unappreciated. It is being for her what you need her to be for you.

The first date became the first of many dates for them. They continued dating throughout their marriage. But this first date was perfect. Everything went according to plan. They were seen together every day since that day.

And now, he was gone—her first, her last, and he had become her everything. And now, at this very moment, all the sweet memories had flooded her soul, and she began to cry. We all began to cry. Even I, but yet they can't see me. Like an uninvited guest at dinner who does not know when to leave, how could I *still* intrude on something so loving, so intimate, so personal, and not feel guilty for this intrusion into their playground? Nevertheless, I dared not leave. I could not. Like a bee drawn to honey, like the hummingbird drawn to the nectar of a flower, in spite of myself, I stayed. I stayed.

Everyone on this playground reached out a hand or a hug to console her. The Courageous Gentleman reached into his back pocket and pulled out a handkerchief and handed it to her to wipe away her tears. How had he died? I didn't know.

But as if she was reading our minds, she fought back the tears and continued her story, and I found out how he died. The question would soon be answered. As she continued through her tears, she said, "I became a professional ballerina, touring with a great American company. He, through hard work, soon came to own his own meat packing company. We were in love. Everywhere I performed, he was there. He would either fly in or drive, depending on where we performed. He never missed a performance. Life had been really good to us. Of course, we had our problems like most couples do, but love really conquers all, and with him, I always felt loved.

"After every performance, he would meet me backstage with a single, white rose. Over the years, I must have received thousands. It was early in our marriage when we decided to have our daughter, and the ballet company allowed me the time off for her birth. The single, white rose continued throughout my pregnancy, even though I was not performing. This single, white rose had become his signature demonstration of his love and admiration for me. I adored each rose as if it were the first.

"After our daughter's birth, I continued dancing, and in the first few years of her life, she traveled with me. It was hard, but he, too, was always there. I was happy. We were happy. Everything was not only picture perfect but *was* perfect.

"A ballerina's career is not a long one. Each performance takes its toll on the body. I knew it would not be long before I had to hang up my shoes. We were performing near our hometown. He was running a little late because of a business meeting. I knew he would soon come to meet me, and sometime during my performance, I would look out into the audience and see him in his seat, the seat where he would watch me from, the seat I knew when I looked toward, I would always receive a smile, the seat I could always see him mouth the words, "I love you." This was our seat.

"But this day at this performance, that seat went empty. I worried for a moment, but like any performer knows, in spite of your worries, the show must go on, so I went on. Near the end of my performance, I always performed one of my signature moves. It is the move I have performed a thousand times, and it had become our move. It's the move that lets him know the show is about to end, and the move that lets him know it is time for him to get up from his seat and meet me backstage.

"That night, as I performed our move, I glanced to see if he was watching me from our seat, and I realized he had not been there. And this time, as I finished performing our move, the move I had performed so perfectly a thousand times, somehow, this time had a flaw, and I fell and twisted my ankle. I got up in pain and gave a curtsy and a bow as the curtains were drawn. As usual, the crowd cheered and roared and stood in ovation for our performance, and they continued standing as the curtain reopened and closed again. In my soul, I knew something was wrong. I could feel something just wasn't right.

"After the show, I found out just before the third act of a four-act performance that a phone call was made to our production manager. On the other end of the phone was the city police department. They were calling to deliver a bit of tragic news. There was a two-vehicle accident. A truck driver apparently fell asleep behind the wheel of his eighteen-wheeler and tragically hit another vehicle, killing the driver instantly. The other driver was my husband."

Once again, she brought us to tears; once again, I have intruded into their playground. Can there really be a love so honest, strong, and true? Once again, I feel guilty for this intrusion into their playground, but as I get up to leave, I know in my heart of hearts I will be back again and will quietly sit nearby to watch where the old people play.

Chapter Two

THE COURAGEOUS GENTLEMAN

I returned to the playground today, and I noticed that a few of my friends are not here. Will they come out to play today? I wonder if they are just running late. I soon learned from my other friends that a few of our friends had scheduled doctor appointments and won't be playing with us today. Doctor appointments and sickness seem to occur often on this playground.

Who am I fooling? I call them my friends, but they can't really see me. I am in their presence but not in their crowd. But once again, I intrude and take my place nearby.

Today, Ms. Red remains silent. She has already shared of herself with us, and like a finely orchestrated symphony, each instrument must take its turn, and so the Courageous Gentleman begins.

What will I learn about him, from him, through him? Each silver cord that runs through his hair tells me he has seen much and knows much, and his head is filled with silver cords. His skin, too, is folded with wrinkles, and yet there is something about his grin that makes him seem somewhat boyish. He walks with assistance from a cane, and every time he moves, I can see his pain. Yet in spite of the pain, he walks. Yet, he can't see me.

I wonder what happened to him to have caused him to use a cane's assistance and began to intrude in his conversation. I listen, and boy, do I listen! Today's order is the same. My friends order coffee, a biscuit, and conversation. Of course, I order a full breakfast. I must have a reason to stay around on their playground.

He tells us that his great grandparents were Irish immigrants who had moved to America for a better life and that he is an American, the fourth born of ten children.

His family had to escape from some of the cruelty they were facing in their homeland. When they first arrived in America, they were extremely desolate and lived extremely poor lives. Although many immigrant families tried to hold on to their homeland traditions, many of the families who had come to the "land of the free" assimilated and tried to fit in.

Their family was one of the first families that had arrived from Ireland on the American shores in New York. I wondered how he got so far south in Louisiana.

He continued his tails of the racial tension that existed during that time, and when immigrants tried to hold on to some of their home country traditions, they faced harsh and deadly treatment from those who thought America belonged to them. Houses were burned, families were killed, women were raped, and even children were killed. For this reason, most immigrants assimilated into American culture and traditions and even changed their names, but I guess when your name is O'Reily, assimilation becomes almost impossible.

I learned that his grandfather moved down south and was able to buy a piece of land that served as a cotton plantation. Even though in America the racial tension was extreme, because of the color of their skin, they were able to assimilate. Some other immigrants of color were not so blessed.

The next words and sentences that would drop from his lips will begin a discourse of some of the not-too-distant history of the African American people. And for some reason, I believe that the stories he will tell us will not be tainted.

"My great grandfather had slaves, but because he was from Ireland and had escaped from much hatred and cruelty, he refused to give in to the ways many plantation owners treated their slaves. There were very few like my great grandfather. Most slave owners were harsh, cruel, diabolical, and downright evil in how they treated their slaves."

In my youth, I may have been offended with his conversation, but right now, there is no offensiveness in the truth. So, I listen with inquisitive ears.

He speaks, "There is no America without the contributions of immigrants, including blacks. We are more than the color of our skin. How could a man have owned another man?"

I began to silently cry, but they can't see me. I cry because my ancestors have become the topic of his conversation with us, and as this white man would tell it, he reaffirmed through his own family's history the atrocities and cruelties perpetrated on the lives of African Americans in American history. Silently, through my tears, I say "thank you" to him for sharing this part with us.

"I grew up on this land, and we still own this land today," he says. "Today, it grows sugarcane." I have just learned that my friend is a sugarcane farmer. He begins to tell us of life on the farm raising horses, pigs, cows, and other animals.

He begins to tell us of a childhood full of love and family and how, as a little boy growing up in the south, he knew besides being a sugarcane farmer, he would be called to a greater cause and purpose.

He remembered growing up with black folks but noticed how they were treated differently than white folks, and he would often ask his parents why. He remembered seeing men on horses clad in white robes and hoods parading through town. He never saw what they did, but he had heard stories. He knew in his gut it did not feel right. His grandfather always told him to trust that gut feeling.

He remembered playing on the farm with a little black boy named Jim. Jim and his family lived on the farm with them and would help his father during the sugarcane season. During the rest of the year, he would help with other farm jobs. When the Courageous Gentleman and Jim were not working on the farm, they would play tag, skip rocks on the water, go fishing, catch frogs, and all the things little boys do. This is what they did in the summer months.

He continues: "Let me tell you about an incident that is forever etched in my mind. Things of this sort were usual for colored folk while

I was a boy growing up in the south. I remember this so vividly as if it were yesterday. Jim Jr. was going away to his grandparents for a couple of weeks in the summer. His grandparents lived about fifteen miles away in the next town. During those days, hardly anyone had cars, let alone colored people.

"We had to be about ten years old at the time. The mailman used to travel to the nearby towns delivering mail in his own vehicle. He took these opportunities to make a little extra money. He would charge fifty cents for a round trip to anywhere he delivered mail. This allowed people without transportation to be able to travel with ease if they wanted or needed to go to the nearby towns. His vehicle was usually packed each day. In those days, mailmen were not paid very well, and by charging riders, he could feed his family.

"I stood outside waiting with Jim Jr. since I would not see my friend for a few weeks. I really hated to see him go. After all, he was my best friend. When the mail car arrived, Jim Jr. smiled and waved goodbye. He reached into his pocket and handed the mailman his fee. The mailman got out of the car and opened the door for Jim Jr. All of a sudden, the white people began to say that they did not want to ride in a car with a nigger and would never sit next to one. The car was full, and Jim Jr. would have to sit next to at least one white person. The mailman had a dilemma. He did not want to miss out on a whole fifty cents, and he could not insult the white passengers. So, he cleverly got into the driver's seat and moved to the center. He told Jim Jr. to get into the driver's seat. Jim Jr. looked puzzled and said that he couldn't drive. The mailman told Jim Jr. that he would not be the driver. He was only sitting where he did not have to touch a white person other than himself. The mailman started the car and drove from the middle seat.

"I could only have imagined how hurt and ashamed Jim Jr. must have felt. He was only a boy. He was talked about as if he did not have any feelings at all. My smile turned into a frown. I walked back to my house and cried. I told my father what had happened. I could not understand why no one would sit next to Jim Jr. We sat at each other's tables.

We sat next to each other as we fished. Being next to Jim Jr. and touching him was second nature to me.

"During school days, I noticed that I rode the bus to school, while Jim walked to another school, and I noticed how whenever the bus passed by the black kids walking to school, some of the white kids on the bus would stick their heads out the window and spit on the black kids. I would ask them why they did this, and they would respond by saying, 'Because they are colored.' I always waved at Jim as we passed, and he always waved back. One boy on our bus addressed me as the 'nigger lover.' One day, while riding the bus, the boy called me the 'nigger lover' and poked his head out of the window and began spitting about the same time I stuck my head out to wave at Jim. He spit on Jim, and Jim began chasing the bus as the other kids on the bus laughed. I walked up to him and hit him in the nose, and he started crying. It was that day when I learned what a coward was.

"My slugging the white boy in the nose did not sit well with the bus driver. He pulled the bus over to the side of the road and made me apologize to the white boy I slugged. The bus driver also sat me down in the seat closest to him for the remainder of the trip to school. Once at school, the incident was reported to the principal, who at once called my father to pick me up. I remember the principal saying, 'Mr. O'Reily, you need to straighten out your son and teach him how things go on around here.' My father responded by asking what was going to happen to the boy who spit on Jim. The principal said that the other boy was of no concern to my father and that he should worry about his own son.

"I could not attend school for three days, and the bus driver did not want me to ride his bus for the remainder of the school year. He told my father to let me walk to school with the niggers. My father told the principal that he did not know what kind of person and principal he was. My father told him that he did not care about all kids but only a certain few. He told the principal that he shouldn't be a principal at any school.

"My father was a big, strong man who stood about six feet five inches and weighed about 250 pounds. As we left the principal's office, he was visibly shaken. On the ride home, my father barely said a word. As a matter of fact, he spoke no words at all. The silence nearly killed me. The only sound I heard was the sound of my breath quickening, for my heart was pounding in my chest. What was he thinking? Was he angry with me? Was I to be punished for my actions? I knew he was angry because I had seen him angry before. But this look truly scared me. I was about to find out what this look indicated really soon.

"He began to pound on the steering wheel, and the next thing he did frightened me even more. 'I could kill that principal right now!' he said. Why had he become so angry about this incident? What had caused him to utter words I'm sure he really didn't mean? Or so I thought. As I grew older, I would learn that my father loved Jim's father, Jim Sr. At that time in our country, race relations were at a boiling point, and my father often felt he was residing in a place where he did not belong. He should not have had to defend his love for Jim Sr. He should not have had to hear from his neighbors that he was a nigger lover. He should not have had to defend his decision to pay Jim Sr. an honorable wage for honest work. He should never have heard the question, 'Why do you allow your son to play with that colored man's son?'

"My father actually believed that maybe in his generation hatred, racism, and bigotry could be stopped. He was determined that the next generation, my generation, would not live in a world where a man was judged by his skin color. Coming from the north, my family had faced bigotry and racism, but not to the extent it was in the South toward blacks. I had never heard or witnessed so much hatred, and it was hard for me to put my heart and head around it.

"By the way, Jim Jr. and I were known for fighting while growing up together. We got into plenty of scraps, and all of them were because of the name calling. We never lost a scrap. Jim Sr. had taught us how to fight.

"Dad finally turned to me and angrily said, 'You have to stop fighting with your hands and learn different ways to express your anger and disapproval of racism and bigotry.' I had also thought that violence must be met with violence and hatred with hatred. As I grew, Jim Jr. and I fought extremely hard to keep our friendship strong, but times were hard, and as we grew, more and more strain was put on our relationship.

"When I went off to college, Jim Jr. had to stay behind and work in the fields to help support his family. I had a chance to go up north where my family had come from to study. There I had a chance to see more of the United States. It was as if I lived in two Americas—the liberated North and the conservative South; the free North and the racially, tension-filled South. Change was coming, and the South seemed not to be ready for it. I was ready. I became involved in a lot of civil rights movements. The right for equality in America to all Americans is vital to the survival of America.

"In college, I took business courses since my plans were to learn how to improve my family's business. I wanted to learn more modern advances to make our business more financially secure and profitable. After college, I stayed up North a few years, married a beautiful girl, and had our first male child. I worked in the world of finance, learning how to build a business using innovative ways in order to make a business successful through investments. I always knew that one day I would move back home and continue the family business with new ideas of expansion. I just didn't know it would be sooner than I expected. I had been away for fifteen years. Jim Jr. and I had virtually lost all forms of communication. I should have written or called, but life began happening, and the days and time just seemed to fly. Soon it was fifteen years later, and I had changed.

"While up North, word came to me that my father had been diagnosed with cancer. It was at this time that I decided maybe it was time to move my now small family back down South. I had already prepared my wife for what to expect in the South. It was not that the North was free from racism and bigotry, but it was that the South seemed more bitter toward the changes that were happening and more willing to hold on to the old ways, even to their own detriment and destruction. My son was still too young to understand, so I just determined in my mind I would protect him as much as I could from the hatred. I had read and seen on news reports some of the things that were going on down South while I was away, but I was truly not prepared for the things I now saw in my fifteen-year absence.

"There had always been a separation of the colored and the whites when I was growing up, but now I started noticing the signs 'Colored Here,' 'Colored Only,' 'White Only,' and 'White Here.' These signs were everywhere. The fight for equality in the South had brought out the worst in white folks.

"We had loaded up all of our stuff on moving trucks and were following behind in our car. We made many stops along the way. In some places we stopped, we saw coloreds eating with whites, but as we moved further south, we noticed the signs, 'Colored Only, White Only.' I noticed how the 'Colored Only' signs hung over the most substandard, filthy, conditioned facilities and areas. Why had I not seen where these signs hung before? While growing up in the South, I had never noticed them. Why were they allowed to still be hung up in public places?

"I began to ask myself how Jim Jr. was doing and if he was happy living in the hard South. While growing up in the South, I knew Jim Jr. was a fighter and didn't take much from anybody. I guess you are all wondering why I had never returned home until this time. My parents came up North to visit us a couple of times a year. They loved the part of the country that was home to my father's ancestors. We never got a chance to come back to the South, and before we knew it, fifteen years had passed.

"As we slowly approached our family home on our family land, I noticed a boy who looked like Jim Jr. Was this lad his son? Was this the son of my childhood friend? While I had been away, I realized that Jim Sr. and my father had become big heroes. They both stood up for what was right to do. How could Jim Sr. maintain such grace and dignity under so much hatred and discrimination and still somehow hang on to his manhood? And how could my father maintain their strong relationship in spite of the times? I honor Jim Sr., and I was so proud of my father. They were real men.

"The young lad ran to the house that was built on the land that my father had given to Jim Sr. so he could own a house for his wife and children. Jim Sr. had built that house with his own hands. It was a two-story, colonial style with a porch that ran around the house. The young boy soon returned, running toward our car. Standing on the porch was a man who looked like Jim Jr.; it was Jim Jr.! I immediately stopped the car, jumped out, and began running toward him. Even though it had been fifteen years, I knew it was him. I ran as fast as my legs and feet could take me. And Jim Jr. by this time had jumped down from the porch and was running toward me. While running, my feet got tangled up, and I felt myself falling, but before I could hit the ground, Jim Jr. had made it to the spot and caught me. This felt familiar. We were always catching each other before we could fall. This man, this colored man, this black man, was my best friend. We embraced and cried, and all of a sudden, all my childhood memories came flooding back to me. We had spent almost every day for eighteen years together, and here we were in the middle of this field, our field, embracing and crying—two men, two full-grown men, two lives, two souls. Life had separated us. Life had brought us back together as men. A lot of life had happened in those fifteen years. A lot of changes had taken place. But there was one constant, which was our love for each other.

"There was not a day while I was away that I didn't think of Jim Jr. He was the reason I joined the civil rights movement while living in the North. Besides coming home to run the family business, Jim Jr. was also the reason for my homecoming. Even when I was away, Jim was always with me. How had he faired while I was away? Was everything all right with him? How was his father? I would, of course, ask my father from time to time about Jim Sr. and Jim Jr., but it wasn't like asking those important questions for myself, eye to eye with my best childhood friend. It would soon be confirmed that after we refrained from crying and embracing, several things had happened around us. My wife and son had joined us. They had left the car and had come to stand where we were. Joining us also was the young lad who I had seen earlier and a very beautiful black woman. It was obvious the lovely family that stood with us belonged to Jim Jr. Standing together now was my beautiful wife and son and his beautiful wife and son. At the introduction of our sons, who were hiding behind us and smiling at each other, we both were made to cry and embrace again. The flood gates of our emotions were opened. I had often wondered for all of those years while we were away if Jim Jr. ever thought of me. Now I knew that I had always been with him.

"Jim Jr. invited us into their home. We went in without going to our home first to unpack from our long trip. Unpacking could wait because we had fifteen years to catch up on. We talked until early the next morning. Our wives and children had fallen asleep in chairs, on the floor, and any-where else they could sleep. Many hours later, I finally woke up my wife and son. We said our goodnights and headed toward our family home.

"I had almost forgotten the sudden reason for my return home. My father was extremely ill, and I was asked to return home because any day he could pass. I guess subconsciously I wanted to reminisce with Jim Jr. as long as I could. I wanted to laugh and cry about good times while growing up together. I did not want to face my father being so gravely ill. As I walked through the door, my mother greeted us and immediately started crying. The man she loved was dying and was near death's door. My parents loved each other dearly and deeply. The man of my mother's dreams, her rock and her best friend, was dying, and all she could do was cry. We all joined her in her tears. My dad soon called out and said in a soft, weak voice, 'Son, is that you? I've been waiting to see you. Come here, Son,' he whispered. His weak voice said a multitude to me. I knew it would not be long before he would answer the last toll of the bell, and I was going to miss him. This was my dad, my hero, my father. The man who had taught me everything I knew. When I had seen him last, he stood tall and strong. Now as I looked upon him, I saw how the cancer had taken away his strength, and I cried. He turned his head away and looked toward the wall, and I knew he, too, was crying.

"I had never seen my father cry. Even with all the horrible things that had happened to him in his life, I had never seen him cry. He was born at a time when they said real men don't cry. And there we were, crying. 'Son, I love you. Don't you ever forget the lessons I've tried to teach you. Love all men in spite of their color. Treat all men fairly, love your family, love your country, and love God with all your heart. I'm tired now, son. I'll see you after I sleep,' he said. As he spoke, each breath he took was a labor of love, and each word seemed to take more life from him, but he had to speak these words. 'I love you, Dad,' I said as we all retired to sleep.

"If I would have known these would be the last words I would hear my father say to me and me to him, I would have talked all night and all day. He died in his sleep that morning, and we were awoken with a high, shrieking voice from my mother, saying, "My love is gone, he's gone!" As I ran down the hall toward their bedroom, I found my mom kneeling beside the bed with her head pressed on his chest. I knelt beside her, and we cried together. We were soon joined by my wife and son. It was then I started crying uncontrollably. It was then I realized that my wife and son had seen me cry.

"I cried because I realized there would be no days of three generations of men in my family fishing together. I wanted us to fish at the pond that was on our family land. I wanted my father to teach my son how to fish as he had taught me. My son would not have the opportunity to get to really know my father, my real hero, and I cried. Should I have come home earlier? Could I somehow have delayed in any way what was inevitable? I will always wonder these things in my heart, but I also knew it was his time.

"A few days later, we buried my father, and it seemed that the whole city came out for his funeral. Even those who had called him those derogatory names came. My father was not loved by all, but he was well respected.

"It was now time to get back to running the family business. I learned that while I was away, my father had relied heavily on Jim Sr. and Jim Jr., along with all the other hired help to run the family business. Jim Sr. knew all the ins and outs of our business, but my father's sickness and death had taken a lot out of Jim Sr. Within a few months after my father's death, Jim Jr. was where I once was. My other hero, Jim Sr., was now dead. But life goes on, and you grow stronger."

Once again, I have been drawn into the life of another player on our playground, and his story has made all of us run the gambit of every emotion. We laughed, cried, smiled, sighed, cheered, booed, and at times we had even been angered. Angered at America's past of hatred and bigotry, angered at the worst of the great country called America, angered that even today, we have a long way to go concerning race relations. Will America ever learn from her past and try to build a better future for her children? The Courageous Gentleman continues, and I soon learn why I have given him the name Courageous Gentleman. He tells us next of the incident that caused him to come to need the assistance of a cane.

The move back down South was not easy on him and his family, and his relationship with Jim Jr. would face even more challenges than it did before. The Courageous Gentleman's wife had tried to stop him from getting involved in the civil rights movement in the South because it was so much worse there. But it was to no avail, so she, along with Jim Jr. and his family, got involved.

"The love that my father and Jim Sr. shared for each other motivated us to give our best to the equal rights movement. You friends have always wondered what caused me to walk with a limp and the aid of a cane. There were many rallies, marches, and meetings to attend and many causes to defend. These were dangerous times in America to be a colored man and even dangerous for anyone who tried to help the colored man. The police were the perpetrators of many of these crimes. In order for the laws to change, the law enforcers had to change.

"In a peaceful march organized to allow the colored to eat in a certain white only restaurant, the police were called out because the restaurant owner did not want the picketing in front of his restaurant. The marchers had every right to be in front of the restaurant, but the police asked the peaceful protestors to move and gave them only five minutes to do so. I was among these protestors, and I watched as the police began to put on their riot gear, bearing batons, tear gas, shields, and even dogs. They were using all *this* for a peaceful protest. My wife and son, and Jim Jr. and his wife and son were all present. It was a hot day in July, and you could cut the tension with a knife. There were words of revulsion and bigotry flying out from the mouths of the white folks. I could see the hatred on their faces. I could hear the hatred in their racial slurs. I don't know why these words are known as slurs. These words were more violent and vivid than a slur. The smell of danger was in the air.

"Hatred is a strong and devastating emotion, but I grew up believing what my father always said. There is no power stronger than love. I saw the fear written on my wife's face as she whispered to me, 'I think we need to leave and get our son out of here before something terrible happens.' I felt what she felt, except I also felt this time I could not run; we had to make a stand. The five minute time limit that the police had given to us had expired, and the captain once again asked us to disperse. By this time, we had formed lines arm in arm to make a chain, and we were peacefully singing, while some of us just sat down on the sidewalk near the restaurant. Next, the captain asked the riot-geared police who had also formed a chain with shields, batons, tear gas, and guns to advance upon the crowd. And within seconds, there was pandemonium as tear gas filled the air, and batons twirled through the protesting crowd. Protestors were falling to the ground while being beaten by police. I was grabbing my son and wife by the hand and running back toward our car, which was one and a half blocks away, trying to get them to safety. I locked them in the car and told them to keep their heads down, and I then ran back to look for Jim Jr. and his family. Time seemed to stand still for a moment, and I saw the hatred in the eyes of policemen as they brutally beat women and children who only wanted the right to eat at this restaurant where the colored were not allowed to eat."

By this time, I was crying. The Courageous Gentleman had painted such a vivid picture that I could see the panic on the faces of the marchers and protestors. I had even smelled the tear gas. I smelled the blood that flowed onto the streets that day. The Courageous Gentleman had also cried as he recalled this painful event from his life. He continued. "As I ran back looking for Jim Jr., I saw one policeman, and he was using his baton to beat a woman who was trying to protect herself from his ferocious onslaught of anger. I could see his anger with every rise and fall of his night stick."

What had this women done, I wondered, to inspire such hatred and wrath from him? As he spoke, I had become angry, angry that the history of America is a history of hatred for my people, my race, and yet some sectors in America will not embrace it and even deny that point of our history. As of yet, they don't realize the effect it had and still has on our future—America's future.

He continues. "I could no longer watch as this white man who was authorized to uphold the law was himself dishonoring it. I ran toward the officer and the lady and asked what he was doing, and his response was, 'Putting these niggers in their places,' as he looked at me and continued hitting her. I could no longer hold my anger and took away his baton. He took that as an act of aggression on my part and soon started attacking me. I grew up fighting and had become pretty good at using my hands. I had even taken a few self-defense lessons. I was getting the advantage over him when I felt a baton hit me on the back of my head. Another policeman had come to his aid and now was hitting me on my right leg with such force that I could feel and hear my ankle shatter. The next thing I remember was waking up in the hospital with my head bandaged, my right leg in a cast, and my hand handcuffed to the rail of my bed. I was under arrest for assaulting an officer, but those charges would have to wait while I recovered from the severe beating from our local peace keepers. The charges were eventually dropped, but I could not ever forget those images of law keepers blatantly and hatefully disrespecting the laws they had sworn to uphold. Moreover, they looked like me. They really hated black folks, and why? Why? What were they so afraid of?

"While lying on my back in that hospital bed, I began to question where Jim Jr. was. Was he OK? I soon learned from my wife, who was now standing by my bedside, that Jim had made it back to where we had parked and had gotten my family and his family safely home and out of harm's way. Jim had looked for me but thought it was best to get our families out of danger. Because of the riot, three people had been beaten to death. Several others were beaten and trampled upon. Unbelievably, all the blame had been placed on the quiet, peaceful protestors. A few weeks later, after I had begun to recover from my injuries, the state police came on my family's land to arrest Jim Jr. and me. We were both charged with inciting a riot. Can you believe the audacity of these charges? I learned a hard lesson. Hate is a devastating emotion. It is destructive, ugly, and cruel, and it is only love that is able to defeat it. All my life, my father had taught me to love all men, and now everything he taught me had come into question. Why had I not seen the true hearts of some of the people who grew up with me? I knew there was hatred for colored folks. I just did not know the depth of that hate. Being away up North had blinded me to what Jim Jr. was facing while I was away from home.

"I realize now that Jim Jr. has been my hero all of these years. While I was away, he must have felt lonely. I was a white man fighting the cause. He *was* the cause. I could stop fighting the cause any time and blend into society if I got tired of the fight. He would always be a black man in America. He could never blend in at this time in America. And here he was, standing up for his God-given rights. It had become a big part of my life, but it *was* his life, and he fought with dignity and pride. The civil rights movement had spawned a great leader of nonviolence in Jim Jr., when years earlier he would have physically fought for these rights."

The Courageous Gentleman had taken us on a journey, and we enjoyed every stop and detour. Because of him, we have seen the best of America and the worst of America. Because of him, I now know from a walker in history that America has to come to grips with some real truths. I feel a sigh of relief and gratitude and an affirmation of what I had already learned of the America in which I was born and the America I love. I accept and honor Her history. I respect and acknowledge Her present. Although I have to fight sometimes, I'm not blinded by Her future. If She does not learn from Her past, She will be destined for destruction.

While I pondered about what had just happened on our playground, to everyone's surprise, in walked Jim. Jr., and immediately he and the Courageous Gentleman embraced. We were given a chance to meet this giant of a man. But who am I fooling? They can't see me! I am around them, I even listen to them, but they can't see me. They all embrace and cry when they see Jim Jr., and I, too, want to cry and do the same, but not with them, for they can't see me. Thank you, Jim Jr., for not being just a story but for being a real hero. I am emotionally uplifted, and now it is time for me to leave our playground until we play again another day.

Chapter Three

THE ELEGANT LADY

It's a rainy day today on our playground, and yet everyone has come out to play. I guess one never grows tired of feeling the rain falling on their faces. In the middle of sipping our coffee, who will honor us with their history and begin to share of themselves? That question is soon answered when this finely manicured, cultured lady, who wore the glamorous clothing along with the most exquisite diamonds and other jewelry, whose make up was always impeccable and whose hairstyle never had one hair out of place, the lady whose aromatic smell of expensive perfume spoke to us of elegance, began to speak.

This was a lady and a woman, a woman of class. When she spoke, she dotted every *I* and crossed every *T*. Every consonant and vowel sound rolled from her tongue like honey dripping from a bee's honeycomb. She had mastered the articulation of the English language, and we later found out she was fluent in six other languages. She was a world traveler and had dined with some of the great presidents of the United States and leaders of other countries. She had even been the invited guest of counts, earls, princes, and princesses and had been the mistress of a few dignitaries.

It was with great anticipation that we waited to hear from her about her life's adventures and stories. Like moths drawn to the flame of a fire again, we were first drawn in to her by the exquisite way she rolled words from her tongue. Words from her were more than just a way of communicating her thoughts. One could tell she loved words by the way she spoke. One could tell by the way she spoke that she had indeed dined with royalty and was accustomed to their ways. There was an air of sophistication about her that let us know she had been in the company of aristocrats, and yet today, as every day, she loved to play on our playground. Plus at no time as we spent time with her did she make us feel we were beneath her.

Very few of us on this playground had ever been to the places she had been or had seen things she had seen. As she was about to take us there, and we were about to travel to lands and scenes only seen in pictures and magazines, we were eagerly awaiting her every word. This would be my first class seat on a trip around the world, and it only cost me a cup of coffee.

Her story begins as a little girl whose father was an international business mogul who had businesses all around the world. Singapore, France, and Greece had been staples of visits in her infant years, as she traveled there with her parents year after year. It was in her youth that her mother was diagnosed with cancer, and this news would change her life forever. At the death of her mother, her father's grief was only comforted by the love of his daughter. They spent many years alone together traveling to exotic lands and had many adventures. She did not attend any private schools at this time but instead had a tutor who traveled with her and her father. She was the apple of her father's eye. He doted over her and gave her everything her heart desired. She even sat in on a few of his power board meetings. She elegantly tells us:

"At the age of twelve, I knew the ins and outs of my dad's businesses and was poised to fill his shoes one day. Everything was great for me until 'SHE' came along and ruined everything. When 'SHE' came along, I was no longer the apple of my father's eye. He no longer doted over me, and 'SHE' was now the most important lady in my father's life.

"The time my father and I spent together was less frequent, and as a result, my private tutor actually became my full-time, live-in nanny since I was too young to stay home alone. I watched as 'SHE' stole my father's affection from me, and I saw a look in my father's eyes I had only seen when he looked at my mother. I knew that 'SHE' was the cause. My father was in love, and 'SHE' made it her point to let him know anytime 'SHE' could that 'SHE' thought he was spoiling me. 'SHE' thought the way he was raising me would do me harm in the long run, or so 'SHE' *pretended*.

"When they first met, 'SHE' was jealous that he was spending too much time with me and covered her jealousy by telling him this was not healthy for me. 'SHE' said that I needed to develop other relationships, especially since I did not go to school. A feud for his affection soon developed between the two women he loved the most. As the months went by, the feud grew worse. At the announcement of a pending wedding, the atmosphere and climate was so thick you could cut it with a knife. In my eyes, it was bad enough 'SHE' had already moved in, but now 'SHE' would share the place my mother previously filled.

"But dad was a grown-up, and it had been years since he had allowed himself to have grown-up love. In my heart, I knew that my dad would need to find a love that I could not give. But in my heart, I wondered why *this* woman? My dad had dated other women since the death of my mother, but none had ever gotten to the point of engagement. It was not as if I had not heard and seen my daddy cry in secret when my mother died. I knew that my father missed my mother badly. He had his lonely moments. He had his tearful times. He eventually had his dates and dining with other women away from home, and there had even been those who visited the estate. To my knowledge, none had ever stayed overnight, not to mention moved in. So, why had he chosen *this* woman?

"I was not trying to keep my father to myself. I only wanted the best for him. I had seen a few money grabbers and gold diggers come in and out of his life. I only wanted my father to find a true pure love like my mother's love. Although I was too young to remember everything when my mother died, his love for mother was the topic of our many conversations.

"The battle lines were drawn and who would win father's affection was the question. Secretly, without the knowledge of my father, 'SHE' had plotted to have me sent away to a girl's boarding school and had even told me of the plans. The first order of business was to have the live-in nanny fired so 'SHE' could carry out the plots without any eye witnesses to her schemes. This was accomplished by first planting small household whatnots and decorations in the possession of the nanny's things and then alerting Father of these incidents.

"'SHE' began to watch the nanny very carefully and looked for opportunities to get rid of her. Only an evil heart and mind could come up with the evil plots 'SHE' plotted. As the nanny taught me, she had a habit of picking up small objects and placing them back where they belonged. 'SHE' began to use gloves to take and hide these objects until she gathered enough of them to place among the nanny's possessions. Of course 'SHE' knew when the nanny would take me shopping on the weekends. While we were away from home, 'SHE' put her plan into effect and went to Father, who just happened to be at home this particular weekend and said, 'I noticed some of the small décor around the house is missing, and I think the nanny has been taking them.' Father said there is no way because the nanny had been his rock and had been with them for years and had never taken so much as a cent. 'SHE' then said that she had seen her picking up small objects and was suspicious of her.

"Of course 'SHE' knew these items would be among the nanny's possessions because 'SHE' had planted them there. On one of those weekend shopping trips while Father was away, 'SHE' had keys made to every room in the house without the knowledge of Father, the maid, the butler, or the nanny. 'SHE,' who had no access to certain parts of the house, now even had access to the nanny's room. 'SHE' would secretly go in there to rummage through the nanny's things. 'SHE' had even been rummaging through *my* things! 'SHE' convinced Father to search the nanny's room by saying that he really should not want his daughter being in the company of a thief, and who is to say that they are not going into the shopping markets to shoplift?

"Father respected the nanny's privacy and allowed her to lock her door. For years, he had trusted her with my life, his only daughter, and had even went away for weeks at a time leaving me in her care. He trusted her with his own life and could not, would not wrap his head around the thought that his nanny was a thief. To his knowledge, he was the only one besides the maid and butler who had keys to every room in the house. He wondered why 'SHE' suspected the nanny only and not the butler or the maid. But he loved her and had to take her at her word. He wondered how could he, how would he bring up the subject of the missing items to his nanny, so first he called in the maid and the butler who both had the weekend free from work and asked if they had seen any items missing from the house. The butler could not recall any missing items, but the maid recalled lately that several items were missing. The maid just thought that the new lady of the house had put them away for 'SHE' was now responsible for the décor of the house. Ever since the announcement of a pending wedding, 'SHE' had begun putting a taste and touch of her decoration ideas into the home, so she had not questioned any items she saw that were missing."

As the Elegant Lady tells us the story of her early years, we are at the edge of our seats because we find the lives of the extravagantly rich intriguing and devilishly exciting. Here their lives are like an Academy Award-winning movie containing danger, schemes, lies, envy, jealousy, pride, and greed—and that's just the early scenes. We wonder as she continues, what else will she say, and how will this story end?

"After the inquiries of the maid and butler, Father has no other choice but to confront the nanny, but how do you confront somebody you consider to be a good friend, someone you have grown to trust and had never given you a reason not to trust her? He still respected her privacy and would not take his own key and enter her room, so he waited for her return. As she walked into the house, my father asked her to come into his study because he needed to talk to her. He told me to go to my room. I could tell by the sound of his voice something serious had happened. As I passed by the study on my way to my room, I noticed 'SHE' was in the study as well, and an overwhelming sense of sadness took over me. Before I could enter my room, the door to the study was closed.

"What was going on in that room? What did my father and 'SHE' have to say or ask the nanny? I had grown to really love my nanny. She was more than a nanny to me. She had become like a mother. I spent more time with her than with my father. I could talk to her about everything. My nanny had even wiped away my tears as I talked to her of the few memories I had of my mother.

"I purposely left the door to my room open as I tried to hear what was transpiring in my father's study. I could not hear a single thing. About fifteen minutes later, I saw my father, my nanny, and that woman pass my bedroom door just across the hallway from my nanny's room. As my father passed, he asked me to close my door, but I asked him what was going on. I saw tears running down the face of my nanny. He then just screamed at me to get in my room and close my door. I fell on the bed crying. My father had never screamed at me until then.

"They entered my nanny's room and closed the door behind them. The next morning, I was told by my father that my nanny would no longer be my nanny and that my new stepmother-to-be would take over the task of tutoring and teaching me. I tried to ask my father what had happened, but he gave me no answer. With my nanny gone, this heinous woman had no one to watch her scheming and deceitful ways, and soon my father found himself again in the middle and in the eye of two female hurricanes.

"Of course they were soon married. On several occasions, my father saw me being very disrespectful to his wife. But he was never around to see any of the devilish, evil actions or ugly words that were her staple of every day occurrences. 'SHE' was the adult and had played this game for a long time and was a master of manipulation and knew exactly how to pull my strings at the right time and always in his presence. In his eyes, I had become the problem and the source of much tension in our home."

This well-dressed, well-spoken, well-manicured lady was taking all of us on the playground on a first class trip around the world to the most fantastic life story and adventure one could ever live. How could there have been so much living in one person's life? Our eyes and ears begged for more of her life story.

"There were two others who could collaborate and bear witness to her scheming ways and these were the butler and the maid. They had been long and loyal employees of my father before I was even born, but 'SHE' had warned them, all of them, if they ever said anything, 'SHE' would make sure they got fired and would never work anywhere again. They had also seen the look of love for her in my father's eyes, and in those days, indigenous workers stayed in their places.

"I soon learned in life that these indigenous workers knew all the secrets of the houses they worked in. You see, before 'SHE' came along, my father and I often visited the homes of his friends, business associates, royalties, and many other dignitaries. Everybody we visited had maids and butlers, and our social circles were the extremely rich and famous. I was friends with all of their children, and like myself, some were privately tutored, some went to private schools, and some were even part of public schools. I was privately tutored because of the travel my father's businesses required, and after my mother died, he wanted me with him as much as possible.

"At that time, we owned several homes around the world, and each one was staffed with indigenous workers. Some homes were single floor, upscale apartments, and others were multimillion dollar homes that sat on acres and acres of land. My stepmother had become the mistress of all this and was relishing in this blast of glam and glory.

"Soon my father and I had a strain in our relationship. I was no longer the apple of his eye. She had made us enemies. I knew he still loved me, but he didn't like me or the things he thought I was doing, and the sad thing about it was that it was all built on lies. But like all lies and houses built of cards, they soon would tumble down, but the damage was already done.

"The first line of offensive they took was to send me to a private girl's school. This was done so my stepmother could have full and complete access to my father without me around. How could she have poisoned his mind, and how could our years of togetherness have been so easily broken? Was love so blind? I loved and missed my father deeply. I remember the day they both dropped me off at the very expensive, very elegant, very accomplished, and highly recommended all-girl boarding school. I remember the smirk on her face, the glee in her eye as they met with school officials to find out all the criteria necessary for my stay.

"They showed us the dorm where I would reside. I exited the car to enter my new place, the place that would be my home for the next six years. My father talked on the ride from the admission building to the dorm and said to me, 'Baby, this is all for you and for your good. You won't and don't understand it now, but you will one day.' Although I heard what he said, it meant nothing to me, and all I knew was that we were heading down a winding road that would come to be my residence for the next six years or until I became a woman. I hated it. As I departed the car, heading toward the dorm, my father proceeded to kiss and hug me goodbye. I did not stop to receive his affections and went straight into the dorm room and closed the door behind me. I fell on my bed crying as I heard him knock on the door. I refused to open the door, and I heard her say, 'She will be OK, darling, let's just give her time. Let's go home.'

"'Home.' This place would become *my* home. I could hear my dad say through the door, 'Baby, we will call you as soon as we get home.' Then he said, 'I love you, darling.' This was the first time in all my life that I did not feel love from my father. I had always needed his love, depended on his love, and trusted his love. Now I felt someone had sabotaged our love for each other. He just didn't know it.

"True to his word, my father tried calling me the minute they made it back home. The trip to the boarding school was a two-hour trip one way. As the dorm mistress answered the phone in the hall and let me know my father was calling, I refused to answer his call. I refused all of his calls. I did not want to talk to him. What could he say? He already thought this was the best thing for me. This was his decision for me, and I had no say in the matter.

"Sadly, there was someone behind the scenes who was pulling my father's strings. The certain someone was whispering in his ear at night as they lay in bed. This someone was selfish and had her own agenda. I innocently became the target of her schemes.

"My first month of school was horrible, and I cried each night, putting myself to sleep with my tears. I was the smartest girl in the class back home. I was going to show my father that he had made a mistake putting me at that boarding school.

"During that first month, my father called every day. Every day I refused to take his calls. Over the next few days, his calls became less frequent. It took about three months before I took his call, and when I did, I did not have much to say. And to tell the truth, I was starting to like this prestigious all-girl school.

"It had truly become my new home. School had actually become a place where my mind could expand, and I engaged in many mischievous behaviors. There was an all-boy school right across the lake, and there were many secret rendezvous taking place. Female hormones and male testosterones were out of control. We younger girls had not of yet engaged in the behavior. But we loved to hear from the older girls as they secretly sneaked back into the dorm. They told all the details of the rendezvous with the boys. During my first couple of years, I found their stories boring and extremely childish.

"By the time I was fourteen that changed. I was too young to fully understand that in a few years it would be me telling those same stories to some wide-eyed, giggling girls—the same stories I found boring.

"Remember, when I first arrived at this all-girl school, I was twelve years old, and at that age, I found boys to be yucky. Within two years, I noticed my body starting to really change. Bumps grew larger, hips flared, and my menstrual cycle came to pay me a visit. I was now fourteen years old and still too young to get involved with boys but old enough to know my feelings and body were changing.

"As the stories continued, I found I was feeling things in parts of my body that I had never felt before. My father had tried to tell me about this time of my life, and now as I look back, I understand his nervousness. He would sweat, and the tone of his voice would change. I could see his struggle to find words that I could understand and grasp the concepts and meaning of what he was trying to teach me. I now know he wished that my mother was alive to have that 'talk' with me. My stepmother and I never had and could never have had that kind of relationship.

"I learned about womanhood from girls at the school. Some teachers tried to tell us, but the real extent of their teaching was to keep our dresses down and our legs closed. No one was truthful enough to tell us the feelings we would get from the voice of a man, the smell of a man, the look of a man, the kindness of a man, and just about everything pertaining to a man.

"At sixteen, I decided I would have my first rendezvous. There were three times during the school year when we had a chance to see the boys across the lake. These were dances that gave us girls and boys a chance to socialize and get away from the drudgery of being a part of a one-gender school. There was the occasional field trip, but for the most part, we spent the whole time in studies around the campus.

"During this time, the visits from my father and her were few and far between, and although the trip from my father's house was just a few hours away, our relationship was never the same. Every visit was no more than a couple of hours, and of course, she tried to play the role of the good stepmother. I smiled and always found a way to excuse myself from their company, telling them I had plans with my friends.

"At sixteen, I felt I was coming into womanhood or at least what I thought was womanhood. I had never even kissed a boy. I just knew at a few of those dances I had gotten close, but the chaperones were as tight as the president's security service. We were never out of sight of a supervised adult. Dancing with boys at first was just something to do to pass the time, and we even did it just to have something to talk about after the dances were over. We just wanted to hear the other girls say that they saw us dancing with a handsome boy.

"We did get to know all of the boys' names, and they knew ours. We would even call the boys' dorms and ask for a certain boy, and when he was called to the phone, we would hang up. There were many phone calls made without the dorm madam knowing. It was a fact that our dorm madam and the boys' dorm masters went to sleep around the same time each night. They would check on us and make sure we were asleep before they would go to bed. Once our madams and masters were sleeping, the phone calls would begin. We were even smart enough to alternate the nights of calling between us and the boys. The volume of calls would increase greatly right after the dances as girls and boys staked their claims on which boys and girls they liked. This took place because there were not a lot of chances for socialization. By the time the next dance took place, the volume of phone calls decreased, and the fondness we had for each other faded.

"This was the time of innocence where we were too young to be jealous. For example, I once liked a boy named John, but by the time the next dance took place, I liked another boy, and my good friend, Susan, liked John. We were just too young for serious relationships, and we changed the object of our fondness liked we changed clothes. But if the real truth be told, there were a few older girls and boys who seemed to have found true love, and it was understood by all that no one would come between true lovers. Some who found true love are still married today; others had their hearts broken, but these were the lessons of life that we were learning, and we would learn so many more.

"At sixteen, his name was Sebastian. He was the son of a British earl who owned a large manufacturing company that supplied the British military. He had the blondest hair, the bluest eyes, and stood six feet two inches. To me, he was the handsomest boy at the all-boy school."

This was the part of her story where the women swooned and the men said "Oh boy, here we go!" At this time, only the women were on the edges of their seats, and while we all listened, this was the part of her story that some men on the playground wished would be brief. But not me. I was intrigued. I had only seen and heard about stories like this in the movies. Now I was actually listening to a person who had lived this type of life, and yet, they can't see me. She continues.

"It was at a dance that I noticed this handsome boy who I had seen many times and even danced with him a few times at the other dances, but there was something about turning sixteen and being at this dance and seeing him that sent shivers up and down my spine. He had always been a gentleman in my eyes, never trying to put his hands on places they didn't belong as I had seen other boys try at these dances. As I think back, he was the only boy I danced with at this particular dance. The talk back at our dorm was about what a handsome gentleman he was. Even though he was only a few months older than I was at that time, he seemed to carry himself with a little more dignity and pride than the other boys. It was the way he walked, the way he talked, his smile, and his superb use of the English language. You could tell he was the son of an earl.

"We had a chance to converse at past dances, and the conversations were simple and trivial, just small talk, you know. Now, at this dance, I wanted to get to really know who he was. As this dance began, I had already determined that I would get to him before the other girls and try to spend the entire dance in his presence. I actually waited by the door, which I had never done before, and because I was slightly taller and stronger than most girls at the dance, I pushed my way through the crowd and was the first girl standing at the door. When I saw him, some would say I ran, but I would say I just walked fast, and I do recall pushing a few girls out of the way to get to him. I asked him if I could have the first dance and all the dances for that night. To my surprise, he said yes. I had never been so blunt and forward. I guess puberty and raging hormones were to blame. I will never forget the song that played that night. Even though I had danced with other boys before, this dance was somehow different. I felt this night more than any other time that I was beginning to come into womanhood. I was beginning to feel differently about boys.

"As he held me close, the first thing I noticed was how good he smelled. How could I have missed this at those other dances? This smell actually made me dizzy. There were many things that night that I noticed and had never noticed before. I noticed next just how tall he was as I laid my head on his chest. It felt so good being this close to him. I also noticed, as I ran my hands up and down his arms, how muscular he was.

He was gorgeous from head to toe. That night, even the sound of his voice made me swoon. I made sure he was all mine and gave no other girl a chance to dance with him.

"We danced all night with each other, and on the songs we didn't dance, we just sat and talked. He talked about his childhood, and I talked about mine. I must admit that I forgot some of our conservation because I would get lost looking into his beautiful, big, blue eyes. He had the greatest sense of humor as he made me laugh many times. I could tell by his mannerisms that he had been raised by royalty and that this all-boy school had taught him all the proper etiquette required for royal society. Two of the classes we had taken in school were etiquette and the other was dance.

"When you grow up in extremely wealthy families, there are certain rules of conduct and expectations that are required to fit into this uptight, elite society, and you are taught this from birth."

It wasn't until now that all of us on the playground realized just how right she was, but at no time did she make us feel we were beneath her. She put on no airs. She was rich and down to earth, and we loved her. Here I go again, interjecting myself into their space. I am not supposed to be here. This is not my space. This is their play area. This is where the old people play, and I am not there yet. Hearing her talk has just made me excited about having my turn to play on this playground, and if I can live long enough, I will play on this field. I moved closer as she continued.

"Speech lessons, etiquette lessons, dance lessons, music lessons, and studying the arts; my life was filled with these, as was his. We were bred for this kind of life, and I played this role well. As we danced and talked, somewhere along this night's journey, I think I fell in love. Somewhere between the dancing and the talking, I was gone. This was a perfect night, and it was my first perfect night, and I didn't want it to end. But all good things must come to an end.

"As they announced 'Last dance!' I began to wonder how this night would end. Would we kiss? Would it go further than a kiss? I had heard the stories of the rendezvous, and I wondered if this would be my night for the rendezvous, and this caused my heart to beat fast. All I knew was that if he had asked me, I would have said yes. As we danced the last dance of the night, he whispered in my ear and asked me if he could kiss me after the dance was over. Of course I said yes.

"There was one, small corner at the dance just big enough to steal a kiss, and after the last song, we ran to that corner. It was then that he grabbed me and held me close, and then he proceeded to kiss me. This was my first kiss. Many of us girls had practiced kissing a boy on our arms as we would sit in each other's rooms, where boys were the topic of our conservations.

My knees buckled, and he literally had to hold me up. At this point, the chaperone hurried us back to our places. As I arrived back at my dormitory, I waited by the phone in the hallway because I knew he would call, and like the gentleman I knew he was, he did. I dared any girl to get on that phone before me because phone history had taught me that once a girl was on that phone, she was on that phone for what seemed liked hours. We talked about how great this night was and how we really didn't want it to end. As we talked, I thought he was going to ask me to secretly meet him for a rendezvous. I knew from the stories of the other girls the how and where of these rendezvous. I really thought that this night would be mine.

"He never asked. Instead, he asked me to become his girlfriend, and of course I said yes. I was a little disappointed that he did not ask me to meet him, but to tell the truth, I was also scared and very nervous and did not know how to act or feel. I later learned he did not ask because he cared too much about me just to have a casual rendezvous, and he wanted a relationship. For the next two years, we spent as much time as we could together. We kissed a lot and participated in a lot of heavy petting. My body ached for him and his body for me. But we did not cross the line of ultimate intimacy.

"We were now graduating seniors, and there may be more than a lake that would separate us. Besides my father, Sebastian was the only other man I had ever loved, and now I was faced with the fact that life's roads may lead us in different directions. Graduation day happened on a Sunday. Both his parents and mine attended. Seniors at both of our schools had a little more freedom, especially if we turned eighteen, as we both were. During the school year, we could actually leave the school campuses if we returned before the curfew. However, the night before graduation, there was no curfew.

"We both turned eighteen and received large sums of money from trust funds that had been set up by our parents. I even had more money coming to me after I turned twenty-one.

"Our last date happened the Saturday before graduation. This would probably be the last night that we would get to spend time together before we had to part ways. We had previously talked about this night being the night we would cross that line of intimacy and decided this would be that night. The plans were a movie, dinner, and then the moment. We had a few details that had to be worked out to make this date happen. Neither of us had cars, but we both had friends with cars. Being the gentleman he was, he arranged to borrow one of his friends' cars. We decided to do an early movie and dinner.

"This night would be our first and only night together. He had reserved a stay at a five-star hotel about twenty miles from our schools. Dinner was great, and the movie was fantastic. As we drove to the hotel, I was extremely nervous. He could tell that I was nervous and tried hard to ease my nervousness with a couple of jokes. I have already mentioned how he had a great sense of humor and made me laugh. By the time we pulled into the hotel parking lot, my nervousness had turned into antici-pation. Since our stay would be only for one night, we packed lightly. He had placed the reservations in the name of 'Mr. and Mrs. Huffington.' We both looked older than we really were. Our room was on the tenth floor, and as we took the elevator up to our room, he reached out and took hold of my hand. Around the fifth floor, an elderly lady dressed in a beautiful gown entered the elevator and asked Sebastian to push the seventh floor button because she was going to a ball being held on the seventh floor, and she wanted to be early. As she exited the elevator, she said, 'Such a lovely couple. Have fun tonight, kids!' and she smiled. We politely told her to have a fun night as well.

"The room was a suite, and I began to wonder if he had done this before and how many times, but I already knew part of the answer. He previously told me that at the age of thirteen he went to the rendezvous spot for a clumsy attempt at lovemaking. The attempt had been a disaster, and he vowed to make his next time romantic and special. Tonight was that special night. As we entered the room, he allowed me to enter first. He closed and locked the door, putting a 'Do not disturb' sign on the outside knob.

"He was smooth and forever the gentleman. My knees shook, and I wondered if he was nervous, too. His demeanor and soothing voice let me know that this was one area where he had a little more experience than me. He had been down this road before, but just how many journeys I really did not know. I had heard all the stories of the other girls, and now it was my turn to feel what they had tried to describe in words. I had often tried to visualize it, as they would describe in vivid details their love making. Tonight I was not a spectator but a participant. Many a night I spent listening, dreaming, anticipating, waiting for the night of my secret rendezvous.

"We sat on the edge of the bed, and he grabbed my hand and was sensitive enough to ask if I was OK. I was trembling. We then began gently kissing. He kissed me on my neck, and my body began to feel things I had never felt before. I began to quiver all over as he removed my clothes. He was slow but deliberate as he removed my shirt and then my bra. I was exposed to him from the waist up, and I had never been exposed to any man before. He gently touched my upper parts and kissed them as my legs and thighs opened for him. The part between my thighs began to moisten and tingle. I had touched myself there before, but I had never felt this much intense pleasure. This time, it was someone else's hands touching me, and he knew all the right spots.

I now longed for him, ached for him, but he was slow and deliberate, and he knew what he was doing. My opened thighs had invited him to touch me there, and he did. It felt so good, and he was so good. While still touching me, he asked me to stand up, and he smoothly unhooked my skirt, and it fell to the floor. I stepped out of my skirt and was now down to my panties. He undressed himself and asked me to help him with his pants.

"Here we stood in only our undergarments and socks. He softly grabbed me close and placed me on the bed and proceeded to touch and kiss me. I was about to explode by this time, and I don't remember how, but within a few minutes, as I lay there naked under him, and as I reached to touch him, he was naked, too. Our undergarments somewhere between the touching and kissing had been removed. He continued to kiss and touch me all over, and my spot longed for him. Then he whispered in my ear, 'Are you ready?' And I quietly said, 'Yes.' He reached to turn off the light on the night stand and to put on protection. He was slow and deliberate.

"I closed my eyes as I received him and started to moan from pleasure. We built up a rhythm as our bodies moved in unison. He moved faster, and I felt that swelling moment in my body. Faster and faster he moved, and faster and faster I felt better. Suddenly, in unison, we both let out a silent scream. My eyes had been closed all of this time, and I realized I had slightly bitten my bottom lip. I felt extraordinarily great, and he told me he did, too. We got up from bed and showered together and, as we bathed each other, touching all the right spots, we somehow managed to make love again.

"We dried each other and climbed into bed after we put on our bed clothes. As we lie under the cover, he said, 'You are really wondering how I can be so calm, cool, and smooth, and make you feel so comfortable.' He told me that he told his father about his first encounter at lovemaking when he was thirteen. His father told him how disappointed he was and how this act was made for a man and a woman who loved each other and were married. His father told him he was much too young to engage in that act. From that day on, his father began to educate him on how to treat a woman good and right in every way.

"When he turned eighteen, his father told him that he was now considered a man and that he hoped he had learned from his first experience and to please be careful. Sebastian whispered to me 'You were not my first, but you are my second, and the most special because I love you.' I felt at ease now because I knew the answer to his smoothness. I told him I loved him, too. We drifted off to sleep right before we set the alarm clock. We both knew Sunday would be a busy day.

"As we drove back to school, it was still quite early, and the sun was just rising. He kissed me good morning and drove back to his dorm. As I entered my room, my roommate suddenly woke, and by the time I closed the door, she asked me how my secret rendezvous went. She was the only one I had told; you always want to tell someone where you are going just in case something happens. I told her it was wonderful, great, and she sat at the edge of her bed and asked me to describe every detail, and I did. My roommate said she was jealous because secret rendezvous were never that romantic. I slipped out of my clothes and into my other sleeping clothes. I lay on top of my covered bed and reminisced about my night. I suddenly realized that I and my roommate had fallen back to sleep and had been awakened by a knock on the door. There was a phone call for me. It was my father and evil stepmother. As I walked to receive the call, I wondered if they had tried to call me the night before and were unable to reach me. My heart was pounding. Would he ask me where I had been and why I did not return his phone call? To my relief, he and my stepmother had decided not to interrupt me and to allow me to have one more day of fun with my dorm mates before the next day's graduation. This would be the last time we had to have fun together.

"My father told me that he wanted us to do an early family breakfast. Of course, my evil stepmother would come along. I agreed to go because during this time at the school, I had only seen them about six times. There were plenty of phone calls, but only six visits. My stepmother thought it was best not to visit often so I could acclimate myself to school life without any interference, and somehow, my dad had agreed. She could get him to agree to anything, even to my detriment.

"There was some small talk at breakfast. I had changed, and I was no longer daddy's little girl. I had grown into a young woman, and last night's rendezvous had in some way empowered me. My heart now had a new interest, and his name was Sebastian Huffington; he was my new love. My dad had told me that one day I would find a man in some ways to replace the love I felt for him, and I had done this in Sebastian, my first and only love. Remember, I said my first and only love and not my only lover. There were plenty of those.

"Soon after breakfast, it was time to get ready for the graduation ceremony. After the ceremony, I would be leaving to go back home with my parents, and Sebastian would also leave for home. We had tried to enter into the same college, but his parents had insisted that he go to college in England and mine in the States, and since our parents were still mostly responsible for our financial endeavors, they had a lot to say about where we attended school. We sort of knew that after graduation it would have been almost impossible to maintain our relationship, so when we hugged and kissed each other after the ceremony, we both cried. This was also the first time our parents had a chance to meet each other, and it went well.

"Sebastian and his parents couldn't spend a lot of time with us because they had a plane to catch, and my dad, being the ever busy man he was, had to also catch a flight to attend a business meeting. So, we said our goodbyes and headed our separate ways.

"As soon as I got back home, I told my father I was going to find summer work; not because I needed money, but to avoid being with my evil stepmother. My dad traveled a lot with his businesses, and therefore we would be alone together, and I was trying hard not to be in her presence. Acquiring a summer job meant spending less time with her. She even thought it was a great idea so I could learn some responsibility, as if she had any. After meeting my father, she never worked again. The nerve of some people!

"The summer went fast, and I was glad to have found a summer job and even gladder when she accompanied my father on some of these trips. Through letters and phone calls, I learned that Sebastian had also found summer employment at the request of his father. We saw each other only once during that summer when he came to visit for a long weekend trip. Those two days were the best days of my life.

"It was time for college, and I went to a prestigious Ivy League school in the States and Sebastian went to school in England. We continued to write and call, giving details of our every move. We tried the long distance thing, and I would greatly anticipate his calls and letters and he mine, but we both knew it wouldn't last; it couldn't last. I had heard that 'Distance makes the heart grow fonder,' but we were young lovers and had never really experienced life.

"There came a time when I never heard from Sebastian again, and at first it broke my heart into pieces, but soon college life mended that heart. College life was exciting—the professors, the climate, the atmosphere, the student body, and especially the boys, lots and lots of boys. Boys of every flavor, and I planned to try all of them.

"I was always a smart girl, but I also became known as a party girl, and I didn't know how that party girl status would send my life spiraling downward."

While in her freshman year of college, her father sent word that she would soon be a sister to a baby brother. There had been very little contact on her part with her father, even during her freshman year. He tried reaching out to her often through calls and letters that often were not answered or returned. She was too busy living up to her party girl status.

She now had a little brother. During her college years, she made very few trips home and never really bonded with her brother or stepmother, and the bond she once had with her father had been ripped apart. She was a brilliant student in college, and in between studies, she partied. Every subject in school was easy to her, and everyone seemed to love her. She was absolutely the most popular girl on the campus in more ways than one.

To call her loose would not begin to describe how she so hungrily searched for love because having lost the two men she had only loved created a fierce appetite in her for love and acceptance from men. As brilliant as she was in her studies, men used her, and she seemed not to care. In some ways, one thought she was trying to get back at her father for not believing her in the early years about her stepmother. There were even a few secret abortions; everything that was against her family upbringing she at some time in her life disobeyed.

Those college years went fast, and now she was twenty-one years old and about to turn twenty-two. At twenty-one, she had come into her trust fund. She was now a multimillionaire set for life, and she planned to live it or at least what she thought life was. At her college graduation, her family had come down, and she had a chance to spend a little time with her brother. They had not seen much of each other while she was in college, and part of her felt guilty because it was not his fault, and he could not be blamed for who his parents were. Deep down inside, she still loved her father deeply, but hurt had pushed those feelings down.

It was at this point in her conversation that I realized you must say you are sorry when you have hurt your loved one. The words "I'm sorry" go a long way. She decided to go home to spend two weeks with her family at the house where she grew up and to get to know her little brother better. Those two weeks were the best weeks in her life, even better than when Sebastian visited. Her stepmother, having had her own child, had changed for the better, and she was a nicer person. The jealousy she once felt was gone, but even this could not erase what she had felt as a little girl. She needed a caring mother the most at that time, and she remembered and cried.

The two weeks at home went by fast, and she felt it was time to leave and experience the rest of her life. As she picked up her little brother, she cried and wondered if she would ever see him again. Her field of study in college was international studies and news correspondence. She was already fluent in three languages with knowledge of a few others she gained while traveling with her father on business trips around the world. Now she would be jet setting around the world on her own.

In her travels, there were no appetites she did not try to satisfy. There were no cups she did not drink from. There were no limits, no boundaries, no saying "no." She did not sip from cups. She indulged in drunkenness to the fullest. All along her exotic and adventurous travels, there were too many lovers to count. There were dukes, earls, Arabian knights, Indian princes (where she was even part of a harem and had to escape), presidents of countries, high-ranking armed forces men, poets, authors, rich and famous, and all flavors of men.

Yet, as she speaks of all this, there is a sadness in her voice and in her eyes. This beautiful, old lady who had taken us to the most exquisite and beautiful places in her story, from the beautiful country of Dubai to the sands of Arabia to the Greek shores of the Mediterranean to the Swiss mountains and the Ireland countryside, had taken us everywhere, and we hadn't moved from the spots we were sitting. We were spellbound as she recreated the places, the times, the scenes, even the tastes and smells of her many exotic travels. She had given us vivid descriptions and details of all these places, and we hungered for more. And here I am again, placing myself in their world, on their playground, and the real truth is they can't see me; I am not supposed to be here.

She pauses, and we wonder if she will continue, and we wait with anticipation like little baby birds to be fed by their mother as she regurgitates their food. The silence was deafening. It was so quiet, you could actually hear the beat of our hearts, and the strange thing was, it was just one beat. Her story had caused our hearts to beat in unison.

She continues for just a moment to say, "I never got married, and I never had any children." After Sebastian and her father, she never found true love again, and we all shared in her tears as she shared to us the saddest opportunity she had missed to love and be loved. I remember thinking, were our thoughts like our heartbeats as one, as I said to myself these words: "She was always the lover, never the loved. She was always the mistress, never the Mrs. She was always the bridesmaid, never the bride." By the flow of tears from all of us on the playground, even our thoughts had become one. And it's here where she puts a period on her story.

We all leave from our spots feeling drained of most emotions yet exhilarated for tomorrow or the next time we meet on our playground when someone else will take the stage and share of themselves and their story.

Chapter Four

THE QUIET LADY

I decided to take a week off from our playground, and once I came back, I found that many of us had decided to do the same. The Elegant Lady had wiped us out emotionally, and we needed a little time to recuperate. We were all eager today to see who would share their story. Would the Quiet Lady, who only nodded, take the stage front and center? I never found out her name. I knew the others; we now had played enough times that I had come to know their names, but they didn't know mine. Why didn't I just say, "Excuse me, friends, my name is _____." I didn't because I knew in my heart I was not supposed to be here. This was their playground. But to my surprise, the Quiet Lady began to speak. She seemed to be just a littler younger than the rest of this group, or so I thought.

She said these words, "I love all of you, and thank you for sharing your stories with me, with us. I look forward to and anticipate these times we play together, and may God bless you always." And she stops. Is that it? Is that all? I waited all this time for her to share with us, and that's all she has to say? I am visibly angry, but they can't see me. In the moments of my anger, I hear a voice on the playground saying, "You're welcome, and thank you for your quiet, supporting spirit. You began this circle of sharing, and thank you for your acts of kindness every time we leave from playing here."

I had not even noticed, but every time—and how could I miss it? Why had I not seen it before? How had I been so blind? But every time we left playing on our playground, she would hug everybody and hand them a small note. I guess I had not noticed because I never received my hugs or my notes. I now long to have my hugs and my notes, but she can't see me. I sit there and just wish she would acknowledge me, that she would see me. When the voice said, "You're welcome," I did not even look up to see the face the voice came from. I dare not reposition myself because then they will know I've invaded their space. The voice sounded like Ms. Red's, but I can't be sure. But whoever it was recounted the Quiet Lady's story, and it's a quiet story.

Her father was a preacher, so God and the church was a constant in her life. She was the youngest of five children. They all sat on the front row each Sunday while her father preached. She loved to hear her father preach, and as he told the stories of the love of Jesus, she wanted to get to know Jesus for herself. Not only was there Bible study at church, there was Bible study at home before they went to bed each night. The children as well had to share Bible stories at Bible study time.

She loved her parents but especially her father. In the pulpit, he was larger than life, and at home, he was the same man he portrayed in the pulpit. He would help around the house and had made it a practice to tuck the kids into bed and kiss them goodnight, and always by his side was their mother. They lived in a modest, three-bedroom house with a den, kitchen, and dining room. The siblings were composed of three boys and two girls. The three boys slept in one room and the two girls in another, and of course Mom and Dad in the third bedroom. The girls' bedroom was next to her parents' bedroom, and so in the quietness of the night, if they were quiet enough, they could hear their parents talking in the next room.

Her father and mother would always kneel down together and pray before settling into bed. She had heard her father pray many times at church and at the family meals, but it was her mother's prayers she loved the most, and here is how they went: "Dear God, I thank you for all the good and beautiful things you have given us, and I pray I will never take them for granted or use them in ungodly ways. I thank you for a loving husband who is my best friend and for using me as a vessel to bring five little blessings into the world, our children. Protect them from evil, and help us to give them a love for you, and help us always to model your love in front of them. Help us to show them who you are in everything we do. In Jesus' name, amen."

Her mother cried as she prayed because she was happy. Her father was happy. The children were happy. Her father preaching allowed her mother to stay home and help rear the children. Her father had showed all of them how to either treat a woman or how a woman should be treated.

They were not rich by any stretch of the word. Ms. Red would switch from third person to first person as she recounted this story, "But we were loved, which made us feel rich. We were a family, and I loved it. Like every family, we had our problems, and I often heard my parents disagree, and we knew Dad had the final say as the head of the house, but we also knew Dad respected Mom's opinions as they came to a final agreement as one.

"I remember one day in particular when I began to really like boys; I was about sixteen years old. If the truth be told, my body was that of a much older woman, but I still had the mind of a sixteen-year-old. This often attracted the attention of a few older young men who were in their late twenties. One day, at our local high school football homecoming game, a young man, who was twenty-six years old, approached me and asked me my name. He did not bother to ask me my age because he assumed I was older than I really was. I never revealed my true age to him. These were the years of innocence, as others on the playground had already noted. Older young men were known to marry younger ladies, and of course, I really thought I was a woman. He was on break from his first year in medical school and had come back for his alumni game.

"He was so handsome and tall. My mom and dad only allowed me to go places if I would agree to take my little sister along. At that time, parents knew children would not do anything inappropriate with a younger sibling present. Younger siblings in those days would run and tell. Reluctantly, I would drag her with me. Sometimes she really didn't want to tag along because she found boys to be quite yucky at this time, but that would soon change, as I always told her.

"The handsome, young man would soon be traveling back to school. I had told him I was a senior at the local university and would love to correspond through mail at his request. My mother knew immediately about this young man and at first saw no need to alarm my father. Four months of correspondence suddenly came to a boil when my father, who was never home during the day, came home for lunch just as the mailman arrived and handed him the mail. Holy Jesus, trouble was on the horizon. My father found in the mail a letter addressed to me from the handsome, young man.

"My mother told me for the first time when I was an adult with children that my father's first intention was to go to school and check me out to address this issue, but she talked him out of doing this. Instead, on that day, my father did not go back to his church office but waited on the front porch for me to come home from school.

"Of course, my father had already read the letter because that's what parents did in those days. There were no kids who dared say to their parents, 'Dad, Mom, I don't have enough privacy in this house.' There was no such thing as kids having privacy in their parents' homes and doing as they pleased. Today, things have certainly changed. Parents don't even know what's happening in their kids' lives.

"As I came up the front walkway, I had the biggest of smiles on my face because Dad was on the front porch, waiting. He had never been home this early before, and I noticed my smile was not returned. Something was wrong. I thought something terrible had happened until I saw that he had my letter in his hand, and then I knew. I heard my father say that we needed to talk and he proceeded to ask me who the young man was and why he was writing to me. The letters were actually quite supportive and encouraging as the handsome, young man talked of how he wanted to get to know me better and how he had come from a Christian family. His father was a minister as well. From the letter, my father told me he seemed to be a fine, young man, but that was not the problem. Why was he writing his sixteen-year-old daughter?

"The first words I said to my father were that mother knows. This seemed to startle him, and he asked Mom to join us in the den to talk. As my mother entered the room, my dad asked her what she knew about this, and her response was everything. My father then asked my mother why he was not told about this, and my mother's response was 'Honey, if you think we women don't ever share secrets that we keep from fathers, then you are fooling yourself. Not only have I known, but I have known from the beginning.' My father asked who the young man was, and I told him that he was the son of a minister and that I met him at a football game. This young man had grown up in the same city where we reside, had finished college, and was in his first year of medical school. My father asked how old he was, and most importantly, was he aware of my age. I had to come clean to my father and tell him I told the young man I was a senior in college.

"I had never before heard my father's voice rise to this fever pitch anywhere but church when he preached, but with a fever-pitched voice and anger in his eyes, he turned to my mother and asked her how she could condone this type of thing. My mild mother, my quiet disposition mother, my humble, submissive mother told my dad in an equally fever-pitched voice to not question her about this matter until he could do it quietly and rationally and proceeded out of the room with me in tow.

"As we left, I could tell my father was totally shocked and caught off guard. I had never before seen him speechless. I had never seen my mother and father like that before. There had been disagreements, but one thing my sisters and I knew from listening to them at night was they always worked things out before going to sleep. I felt that there was no problem their love could not conquer, and that was the foundation my parents had built for all of us.

"It seemed at times that my dad did not realize I was at the beginning of womanhood. My dad had preached many sermons over the years about love between a man and woman and what God's expectation was for all men, but more than that, my dad had lived the sermons he preached before us. My mother had already tried and had successfully explained to me womanhood as it relates to men. I remember my first menstrual cycle. Mother explained what was happening to my body, and she held back nothing. My dad would now just have to trust the words he and Mom taught me, for these words had taken root in my heart. I wanted to walk into their room and tell him this as they began their nightly bedroom talk. Here are the words my mother said to my dad: "'Honey, I am surprised by your reaction to me and our daughter. Mothers and daughters have kept secrets from their fathers for years. Just call your mother and sisters and ask them. I even know the lie she told that young man and told her I expected her to do the right thing, and I gave her the space to do it. Sweetheart, if you haven't noticed, our daughter is only one year younger than I was when I married you, and she is not our little girl anymore. Baby, God gave us these children to provide for them, body, soul, and spirit, and to do as much that is in us to protect them from as much as we can. If there is one thing big bad fathers and ever loving mothers can't do is protect them from relationship heartaches. It's a part of life.'

"I loved that as my mother always talked, my dad seemed to always listen, and because of how Dad worked as a minister, he was not the talkative one at home. That was Mom. At home, my father had a quiet strength. My dad was a real man. As my mother continued, I could have sworn I could hear my father crying as she began to recall to him their dating years while she was yet in high school.

"My dad was eight years older than my mother. They were both preachers' children who lived in the same city. Their families met often for dinner. She reminded him that when they first met as children, she did not like him at all. He was the same age as my mother's older brothers, and they were best friends. She thought my father was quite nerdy.

"My mother continued. 'I remember when I turned fifteen, you had already finished college and had gone off to seminary school to prepare yourself for a life of ministry. You had come home for the weekend, and this was the same weekend your family was scheduled to have dinner at our home. When you walked through that door, my mouth almost dropped. You were no longer that nerdy-looking boy I didn't like. You looked quite handsome in your sport coat and slacks. Even my little sister commented on how cute you had become. I had matured a little myself, and I caught you taking second and third looks at me. I even remembered how you had told my parents that I seemed to be growing up into a fine, young lady. I noticed you, too. You were beginning to look for a wife you could share you love, your life, and ministry with. Your father was a preacher, and my father was a preacher, so we knew firsthand as children the lives that were expected of us. I recalled you even asked my father if it was OK for us to start corresponding with each other. My father was a little concerned with the age difference but trusted in the great, young man you had become. Two years later, we were married.

"'While married to you, I was allowed to go to college, and soon after, God blessed us with children.' As my father remembered the events, I knew he was crying, and then to my shock, he called me into their bedroom. I rushed in to hear him say, 'Honey, I know you and your sister have been privy to hear the many late night conversations your mother and I have, for we, too, can hear your whispers and conversations.' My dad was crying real tears as he spoke to me. I had seen him cry many times before in his sermons and for the lives of the people of the church. He had baptized their children, buried their loved ones, performed their wedding ceremonies, accompanied them through their good and bad times, but these tears were for me, his oldest daughter.

"He began to wonder where time had gone. What had happened to the little girl in pigtails and bobby socks, the little girl who thought her dad was the only man she would ever love, the little girl he would rock to sleep when she ran to his arms after the boogie man paid her a visit through a bad dream, the little girl that would bring all her broken toys to him, and he would fix them, the many tears he would wipe away due to itsy bitsy problems upsetting her. It was now that this little girl would turn to wipe away his tears and say, 'Dad, I will always be your little girl, but one day, someone else's wife.' And then I heard my dad say, 'I'm sorry, honey, but please do something for me. Please tell the young man the truth about your age.' I told him that I had, and that was the reason he was coming home soon to talk to him.

"I married that young man, and we have five children—two girls and three boys, and my husband practiced medicine at the local health clinic while I stayed home to raise the kids."

I now know why she hugs everybody and hands them notes of peace. It's in her to help feed one's soul, thanking them for their words. These are powerful little gestures that warm our hearts and put a smile on our faces. But they can't see me.

Chapter Five

THE VETERAN

The weatherman calls for rain and thunderstorms today, and I begin to wonder who will come out and play. As I arrive at our place, I notice the playground is almost completely empty. I hang up my raincoat and put my umbrella away. The only one present so far is the Veteran. He has hung his raincoat and his hat. I had never seen him with his hat off, and I notice he has a long, terrible-looking scar that runs from the front to the back of his head. He was trying to hide that scar from the rest of us on the playground. Was there a story behind that scar? I looked at that hat with all of the military lingo and pins. He had so many pins that represented places he had traveled while serving our country.

On one occasion, the Veteran had stopped in to see us while on his way to a Veteran's Day program, where he was being honored. His coat was full of stripes, awards, and medals. In fact, there wasn't any room left for any other medals. There were at least four Purple Hearts. All of this told me that he was a great soldier. There were those on the playground who applauded and saluted him on this Veteran's Day, and I was one of them. Then he soon found his way to where the others played, and I was not invited.

Once again, I took my place on my bench overlooking the playground, and I waited to hear the story behind that terrible scar. He had a very raspy voice, and he pulled a cigar from his mouth and talked between puffs. We often told him he shouldn't smoke, but he would respond that if the war didn't kill him, nothing else could, and he had been smoking cigars since he was seventeen years old and was now ninety.

For a man who had been to war and had smoked for all those years, he looked like a man in his sixties and was in great health for an old man, except for a hearing aid. Everything else seemed well, and although he had that scar on his head, he still seemed to be able to think clearly. He began to talk of war and told us to remember that all was fair in war, which really meant he had seen and experienced his share of tragedies and had the scars to prove it. He had even, at one time on our playground, opened up his shirt to show us a chest that had been sprayed with bullets during one scrimmage of war.

He was sixteen years old when he became a soldier in the military. He had lied about his age and was allowed to enter. He was delighted to serve his country. He was a true patriot who loved America, and "Land of the Free, Home of the Brave" was an inscription he wore on the side of his cap. He loved basic training and was the top private in his troop. He could shoot the flea off the back of a mangy dog a hundred yards away and had learned how to shoot while hunting with his father. There was nothing to do in the town where he grew up. All this town had to offer was coal mines and steel factories, so he decided the military was the life he wanted to live. He wanted to become a soldier's soldier. If there was someone made for war, it was him. With the gruffest voice you could ever imagine, he began to speak. His tone was sharp and to the point, as if he was speaking to young, inexperienced troops.

I had uncles who had been in the military, but I know nothing, except what I read in books and had seen in pictures and documentaries. But he, who sat with us, was a real American patriot, soldier, and hero. He began by saying, "Let me tell you stories not found in many books. By the time I was eighteen, I was deployed to the front lines. The branch of the military I was in was on the ground. We fought hand to hand combat with tanks and other equipment. I am really blessed to be alive. It is because of war I don't fear death, but it is also because of war that I treasure every minute of life and don't take anything for granted. I have no time for foolishness."

He started describing in vivid details the horrors of war and how he had to learn how to rationalize some of these tragic events he faced and witnessed, and the slaughter, as he called it, of innocent civilians. "Our commanders had also tried to get us to see it as a necessary inconvenience of war. I could never do that because these people were somebody's brother, mother, father, sister, husband, wife, and child. They were not just numbers for news reporters and military reporters to type and to say, 'Five hundred died in a battle insurgence.' These were human beings created in God's image. I was not a deeply religious man, but somehow, this never seemed justifiable, but I did it, and I did it well. I was one of the best, but I soon learned there was a price to pay for being the best.

"I have seen many a man die, many a man cry. I have witnessed brain matter of my fellow soldiers splattered on my face as gunfire ripped through their bodies, causing me to check and see if I had been hit myself. I have had to try and place intestines back inside the stomach of friends and fellow countrymen as bombs tore their bodies asunder. I have seen my comrades feel for their lower body parts that had been ripped away from their bodies, only to tell them minutes before they would die that they had no lower body parts. I have held the hands of men who breathed their last breaths and cried to go home, only for me to tell them, 'Yes, friend, you are going home, but you won't be alive.' I had seen explosions where there was not even enough body parts left to recognize who that person previously was. Only the dog tags were left as identification. I smelled the rotten flesh right next to me while we were pinned down for days in the worst of conditions. You could almost reach out and grasp the thick smoke that filled the air. Worst of all, you could not cough because you did not want to alert the enemy to your location.

"No man should ever have to witness so much death. War is hell. We would sometimes go without food on the battlefield so long we contemplated eating the rotten corpses. The sewage water we drank made us vehemently sick, but that was all we had to drink. Don't get me wrong. In between the fighting, there were some good days, days you would receive a letter from home, days you had enough time in camp to drink a beer and bite into a steak and to listen to a radio broadcast. If it were not for those few days of normalcy, or at least as normal as it could be for war,

I would have probably come back home to America and slaughtered many. It is not the toil that war puts on your body but the toil it places on your mind. No one that goes to war returns back home the same. No one, and if they say they do, they are big liars.

"I had heard the story of many other wars and thought I could handle being a participant, but there is no amount of training one can take to prepare you for the horrors you will face." As he continues, tears begin to well up in his eyes as he recalls the day he longed to go home himself, but he was a long way from home and knew thinking of home would only take away the heightened sense of alertness that was needed for his night of guard duty. He continues between tears and the pulling of his cigar.

"She was the most beautiful little girl I had ever seen. She had black, straight hair, oval-shaped eyes, and she was a daughter of our enemy. I have many stories of how our enemy would use any means necessary to win this war. It was my turn for guard duty, and I had sniper accuracy and the greatest eye sight in our camp. I often wake up even now with night terrors, sweating, yelling, and asking God why on that night was I on duty; why me? The commanders always tried to reassure me only I could have done what was needed to be done that night.

"It was actually early, early dawn, just before sunrise, and in a few hours, I would be relieved of duties. It had been a quiet night, and I was looking forward to a little rest from my heightened sense of alertness. This heightened sense could not be good for your heart, as I could feel my heart racing along with the sweat on my brow. It was a Sunday, and as I walked, I watched continuously and moved so the enemy would not and could not predict where I was. My heart was pounding, my blood was rushing, but my trigger was ready. When fighting time would come, I was said to have nerves of steel with ice cold water running through my veins.

"She was beautiful with her long, straight, black hair, oval face, and oval-shaped eyes. I had seen her coming in the distance through the scope of the rifle and the binoculars that hung around my neck. She was crying, and from the look of her frail body, she hadn't eaten in days. Why was she headed into our camp? Had we destroyed her home in the midst of our fighting? Where were her parents? She was much too young to be out there by herself. This could have been my little girl, and for a moment, I was moved by compassion. Let someone give her some food and a drink of water; that seemed to be all she needed. Once we would have given her what she needed, would we then take care of her at our camp or send her back where she came from?

"The other soldier who shared guard duty with me that night radioed me and asked me if I could see or had I seen that little, beautiful girl. I responded back that I had. The other soldier had a better viewing spot and asked me what I thought she wanted, and I told him by the look of her frail body and tears, some food, water, and maybe a hug. Even in the midst of war, this little, beautiful, big-eyed girl had brought out my sense of humanity at a most inopportune time. I was on guard duty and needed to be alert.

"In the midst of mangled, twisted, bloody human wreckage, I felt a sense of compassion. In times of war, these are senses you have to push way down in the depths of your being. There is no place for compassion and humanity during war, especially for those considered to be your enemy. You become a fighting machine—a thing, not a person. The next words my fellow soldier said to me sent shivers up my spine and tears to my eyes. 'I think she has a bomb strapped on her back.' I had heard the terribly horrible stories of the enemy using hungry, starving, crying children to walk into our camps with bombs strapped to their bodies, trying to kill as many of us as they could.

"'Oh God,' I cried, 'please don't let this happen to me.' I knew we had already shed the blood of many little kids like her, but I could rationalize it away by saying I did not know any I had personally killed. This was now personal, and for a moment, I was being torn apart. Shooting this little girl just didn't seem right, but the needs of the many outweighed the needs of one. He called out to me and said, 'I can't do it. My hands are shaking too much, so you must make the shot.' The answer I returned was, 'Are you sure it's a bomb?' 'Yes,' he said. It was then I knew it had fallen on me to take that shot. I brought the gun up to shooting position, just hoping as I looked through the scope she would turn back from whence she came, but she came moving forward. I was never a praying man but remember asking God to please make her turn back. 'Lord, can I shoot this beautiful little girl who had brought me such a beautiful moment of humanity in all this tragedy? Please, God, don't ask me to do that.' But as she moved ever forward, and I put my hand on the trigger, all my sense of compassion and humanity had been pushed way down in my soul, and I squeezed the trigger. As I squeezed, the machine that war had made of me had taken over. And with sniper accuracy and ice water running through my veins, I dropped her in one perfect shot in mid step, and upon her fall, the bomb went off. I would have hated looking at her face right after the shot, not even five minutes later. I was relieved of my guard duty and was headed for some much needed rest, and having to come down from my heightened alertness, I began to cry and long for home.

"If only the incident would have happened ten minutes later. That is when I would have been relieved of my guard duty. Only ten minutes could have rid me of the albatross around my neck that I still wear today. As I made my way back to rest, the sergeant saw the conflicting paradox of the event and said, 'Son, you saved many a soldier's life today.' I killed this little girl, and I just wished somebody else would have worn this albatross. Ten minutes. I only wished for a different ten minutes. A life can be drastically changed in only ten minutes. Ten minutes was all it took for this event to take place. Ten measly minutes.

"I was never the same after that. Oh sure, I could sometimes find some humanity in the midst of war, yet in the twinkling of an eye, I could turn to a fighting machine, and I was becoming that which I didn't want to become.

"Many of my friends never could fit back into American society after war, and I must admit, my decompression back into society was hard. I saved many lives in the war and killed a lot of people.

"As the war ended, I often found myself trying hard to assimilate back into American society, which was difficult, and the nation, at times, seemed to have forgotten about us. Many of my comrades ended up homeless and unable to get any proper medical help for the physical and mental problems war brings. Soldiers and spouses had gotten divorces, as parents left behind had to take care of family business and children alone. Sons came back home only a shell of what they were before they left, and these parents had to deal with the feeling that their little boys were lost within themselves.

"Before I left fighting, I could not tell how many men I had killed, and for a time, that bothered me, but what really woke me up and stole the peaceful moments of sleep was remembering my beautiful, long, straight, black hair, oval-faced, oval-shaped-eyed little girl. How could I rationalize taking her life? She had her whole life ahead of her. She was somebody's daughter, someone's loved one, and she was gone, and my hands were the ones that had caused that. Ten minutes, I kept thinking.

"I went straight to my parent's home after the war. I hadn't seen them in years, and the reunion was a sad and happy event. Sad because they had grown a little older and so much time had caused us to be nervous for a few days. In those days, I was found to be very quiet and reserved. I had gone to war a child. I had come back home a man. My mother doted on me as if I was still her little boy. She would cook for me, wash my clothes, and clean my room. The room I occupied as a child was left the same way it was when I had left for war. The room had the same childish décor. I asked Mom if I could take down all those childish reminders and put them away. I was not that child anymore, and they only brought back memories of those good, innocent, happy times. I had seen too much in war, done too much in war to want to remember my happy childhood. I had pushed my humanity and compassion so deep down inside of me because I needed to justify what I had done. It took years to bring those emotions and feelings back. Funny thing; even the America I knew had changed.

I remembered as I passed through the airport headed home from war that I received standing ovations and salutes, and people called us heroes. I did not feel like a hero, just a soldier doing his job. I realized later it was just America saying, 'Thank you' for a job well done, and I began to except America's ovations and salutes and would take a bow as I placed my hand over my heart. It was not because I thought I was great, but it was my way of saying, 'You are welcome.'

"I needed help assimilating back into American society, and unlike many of my comrades, I got help. My father especially noticed the difference and would ask me if I wanted to talk about what happened. I didn't want to talk. I was trying to forget. I often frustrated my mother because when we did talk, I only gave one-word answers and would never elaborate on anything. My dad basically just gave me space and said very few words.

"I often woke up several times during the night, screaming and yelling, reliving some of the horrors I had experienced. Each time this happened, my parents rushed into the room to comfort me and waited until I went back to sleep before leaving the room.

"For a few months, they gave me space and time. I knew I couldn't stay with my parents forever, so I would sit at the kitchen table wondering what I would do with my life. For five years, I belonged to the American government. For five years, every day I had to salute men of higher rank. For five years, I was America's fighting machine and had taken pride in being an American. For five years, every day I was told what to do and how to conduct myself and had become dependent on the men next to me, but now I was home, and I felt all by myself. I was lost in America. But unlike many of my comrades, I had a family to come home to.

"Many a soldier came home only to find out their wives and children had moved on and had gone on with their lives without them. Some soldiers' parents had died while they were away, and they went home to empty houses. I was really one of the lucky ones. I decided to try to do activities with my father. I asked my father to go hunting as we had done many times before I went to war. I had not picked up a gun purposefully since I left the war and didn't want to even see a gun, but with these few months of being home with loving parents, I began to feel more like my old self. I decided to go deer hunting with my father.

"I fondly remembered the time I killed my first deer. I was smiling with the widest grin my face could produce as we traveled home to show my mother and younger sibling the feat I had accomplished. I was the older of two sons, with my brother being five years younger than me. Here I was again, spending quality time with my father and brother. My brother had just graduated from high school and was planning to attend college. He was completely different from me and more of a mama's boy, and I was more like my father. My brother liked cooking the food more than hunting it. He had gone on a few hunting trips with us and knew how to handle a gun, but there were times he preferred to stay home with Mom. Since he was headed to college soon, he decided to join us on this hunting excursion. Besides, I knew he just wanted to spend time with me.

"I was totally excited as we got everything packed for our two-day stay in the woods. I looked forward to a good hunting trip. As we arrived at the spot, I was flooded with a lot of boyhood memories and began to smile, but soon the day would take a turn for the worse. While we positioned ourselves in hiding places from the deer, my heart started pounding faster, and I began to sweat. I was back in war, and once again my heightened sense of alertness kicked in. I almost forgot where I was. We always wore camouflage to hunt. When I spotted the deer—the enemy— I took aim and pulled the trigger, hitting him squarely and solely where I aimed, which was in the head. Before he could hit the ground from the first shot, I shot him in the head two more times, making sure he was dead. Without even knowing it, I had rolled on the ground between the trees because I did not know if the enemy was dead. If it were not for the voice of my father and brother calling out my name and snapping me out of the trance, I might have also taken them for the enemy and killed them. The thought sent shivers running up and down my spine, and it was then I knew I needed to get professional help.

"I made calls to state and federal agencies and even to military personnel, trying to find out if there was any help for what was ailing me. I had been in war, and now as I tried to assimilate myself back into American society, the war was still in me. And at times, it seemed as if there was no help for me. There were many hospitals for the physical toll the war had caused, but the mental hospitals had bad reputations regarding their treatment methods. It was apparent that the war had taken some mental tolls on me. I was only twenty one years old when the war ended, but I was an old man mentally.

"I finally found the right help I needed after many failed attempts. I found a psychiatrist who also believed in God, and he believed in the forgiveness of sins and guilt. He truly believed once I could put my guilty feelings of what I had done to rest, I would heal, could heal. He first talked about me sharing with those I loved the horrors I had seen and not keeping all that stuff bottled inside. He told me if I couldn't talk to a person, talk to a tree. I found out many people called his methods unorthodox, especially a psychiatrist who believed in treating through God. There seemed to be times where most therapists' treatments would be diametrically opposed to God, but this psychiatrist believed it was God who created the mind and the power of the mind. He believed one could never be trapped inside his mind, and he had seen many a soldier healed once they learned where to put the guilt.

"The psychiatrist began to explain about what he called the children of Israel who were God's chosen ones, according to the Bible, and how during their lifetime, even as God's people, they had been involved in war. He talked about the grace of God through his son, Jesus, and how Jesus died for us so that he could take away the sin and guilt that sin brings. That is exactly what I needed to hear. I no longer had to live with the guilt. Is war sin? It really doesn't matter, but I don't think so. I began to believe that Jesus died to take away the guilt. This relieved me of the tremendous burden I had placed upon myself."

While intruding and listening to the Veteran, I could agree with him because I, too, am a preacher, and I want to say "Amen," but they can't see me.

The Veteran continues. "This was the beginning of my healing process, and it has been a long, hard journey. I must admit, the first time I shared the horror I experienced with the big oak tree on my family's land—the oak that provided shade in the heat of summer, the oak that I and my girlfriend had carved our names in when we were so much in love, the oak that my mother, my brother, and I would sit under as she read us books, the oak I had seen my mother and father sit under and just talk and steal secret kisses, the oak my brother and I often watered when we couldn't make it home to use the bathroom—that old, faithful oak was the first to hear my horror stories.

"It was not long before I shared everything with my parents and my brother, and we cried. We all cried. The cloud of guilt began to rise and soon disappeared as I started going to church. This process took three long, hard years. Now I was ready to take my place back into American society. Since I knew nothing but war and had not even gotten my high school diploma, I got my GED and enrolled in a local small college to become a writer. I have written three military novels and have inked out a comfortable living writing and traveling to places where I talked about war and anything else I feel like talking about.

"By the way, I married the girl whose name I carved into our oak tree. We have four children, twelve grandchildren, and eighteen great grandchildren.

"I am often asked how I feel about war, and my response is, 'There will be some countries where compromising and talks work. But there are countries where only war brings about change. I love America and would defend her with nine lives if I had nine to give.'"

And today, as he gets up to leave our playground that is now buzzing with activity because everyone else has come out to play and were just waiting for the rain to stop, he receives standing ovations and salutes from everyone. I even stand to salute and clap, and he tells us he is on his way to receive another award to place on an already overcrowded mantle.

I again noticed all the medals and honors he had received, and I, too, am proud to have met him. He tells us as he makes his acceptance speech that he must tell the audience about the God who brought him through the war, even when he did not know who God truly was, and that everywhere he goes he talks of God. And to that, for that, I silently said, "Amen." But they can't see me.

As he began to leave, I said to myself, "The scar, what about the scar? I guess I will find out the story behind the scar another day, and if not, it does not matter because he has just shared for us the essence of who he was. He was the Warrior."

Chapter Six

THE JOLLY MAN

There is only one left on our playground who has not shared of himself to us and with us. He is the oldest in our group. The Jolly Man plays the hardest on the playground because he has the most to forget. Age has taken away his step but not his wit.

He always has a comment and some sarcastic remark as the others shared themselves. When Ms. Red had gotten up to dance, he said, "Pretty lady, you better sit down before you break a leg or trip!" When the Courageous Gentleman talked, he said, "You know, you really broke your leg chasing after a girl who was running away from you!" To the Elegant Lady, he had said, "Let's go get married right now. We are too old to do anything else but rub each other down with muscle rub, but that might be exciting!" And to the Warrior Veteran, he said, "At one time, you may have been able to shoot the flea off the back of a mangy dog, but right now, you are so blind you couldn't hit the side of a barn!"

Every day, as he played on our playground, he was the one who brought the humor and the laughter. Even the way in which he laughed made us laugh. It was the jolliest of laughs that brought water to his eyes. He did nothing halfway, from laughing, to eating, to smiling, to joking, to playing—he put his heart and whole self into everything he did.

There was no phoniness in him; he either loved you or not, and with him, you always knew where you stood. He was the most honest, straight forward person I knew, and he loved hard and he would die for you. He was the best friend you could ever have because he would tell you what he thought you needed to hear and not what you wanted to hear. Don't ask him if what you wore that day on the playground looked good because you may not like what he had to say. Even when he told you the naked truth, he did it in such a way that you kept your dignity and self-esteem. The truth is, relationships determine how well criticism is received. If you know that someone loves you, criticism will be received kindly. If you just let someone who does not love you try to criticize you, there might be a fight. The Jolly Man loved everyone on our playground. He would disagree with you many times, but he was not disagreeable.

Why had he not shared of himself with us? Was it because he was the oldest in the group and allowed the younger players to go first? Was it because he had the most to say? Does quantity necessarily mean quality? Was he just afraid to share with us, or had his moment just not come?

We came to the playground over and over and over again. Days turned into weeks and weeks into months, and at no time did he feel the need to share with us. He had made a few of us angry as we thought it was not fair of him to hear some of our saddest, most intimate moments but had not shared his. We felt he had robbed us. But the truth was, no one had twisted our arms nor asked us to share of ourselves. It was all voluntarily, and this was the nature of our playground. We knew Father Time would one day pay us all a visit and wondered would he share to us, for us, with us his most intimate moments, and would he do it before time came to pay him a visit? Mother Nature already visited many of us on the playground, trans-forming us into old folks. Dentures, support girdles, support bras, muscle rub, hair color, glasses, and hearing aids filled the playground. I don't know what we smelled most like, arthritis cream or perfume.

If, or when, would the Jolly Man share his story had become the big-gest buzz on our playground. One day, he hadn't come to play, and we found out from his granddaughter, who often brought him to play, that he woke up one morning disoriented and confused, which scared her, so she had taken him to the doctor. An MRI was done on his brain, and the doctor ordered him to rest until the results came in. Although he was the oldest on this playground, he still was able to function considerably well.

The next week after his MRI, he came out to play wearing a big, red jumpsuit. We never knew what he would wear to play. He always wore the brightest colored jumpsuits. Was it for laughs, or was he color blind? It probably was a bit of both. Everybody was glad to see him as he exited the car. He shook about ten peoples' hands before he finally made it over to sit and play with us. Everybody knew him, and he knew them. When he finally made it to the spot where we played, he ordered the usual, which was the strongest cup of black coffee he could order, along with a little conversation. The name of every person on our playground rolled from his tongue. This, he had never done before, and we began to wonder if this had anything to do with what his granddaughter told us the week before. It was as though he was making sure he remembered all of us. Man, I should be ashamed of myself, once again using words like "us" and "our," trying to include myself in this place where they play. I know I am not a part of them, but they have become a part of me. I have come to need them; their stories have inspired me, motivated me, and because of them, I have begun not to be afraid to grow old and play here.

What did the MRI reveal, and would he tell us? He just seemed different today, as if he was trying to prove to us his mind was still sharp as ever. I had already known there was some shrinkage of the brain due to old age, and some memory loss naturally occurs. Was he trying to prove something to us or to himself? Today he was extra talkative, as if something had compelled him to share his story. Had the visit to the doctor moved him to share? We began to speculate that Alzheimer's was setting in, and he had become afraid he would not tell his story with accuracy, and this made the urgency of telling weigh heavily on his mind.

The mood turned very serious as he shared what we had already speculated. The MRI showed some deterioration of the brain with a little bit of bleeding. Because of his age, the doctor did not know if surgery would be an option. We all grew sad at this announcement because he was the one who played the hardest and seemed to have the most fun. He was the one everyone would call to make sure he was coming out to play. He could turn the most serious of moments into moments filled with joyous laughter. No one was quicker when it came to saying the right words. Simply put, he made the playground a happier place, and it saddened us to think that one day he would be unable to play. He began.

"We were poor, very poor when I grew up, and unlike most poor children, my parent never hid or could hide how poor we were. There were many nights we went to bed hungry. My mother died while bringing me into the world. I was her and my father's only child. My father tried hard to raise me on his own, but the death of my mother left a hole in his heart that could never be filled, so he began to drink. He became the worst alcoholic. I was very young when he realized he could no longer take care of me. He brought me to live with his sister and her family. They lived only two miles up the road from us. Eventually, my father lost his job as a sharecropper due to his alcoholism. My aunt and her husband were sharecroppers also. They were determined that their three children, along with me, would not join them in the fields and would get an education for the hope of a better life. Most children in the area joined their parents in the fields. Having one more mouth to feed during those lean years was tough, but my aunt and uncle treated me like their own child. I would see my father from time to time as he struggled with his alcoholism. The visits became few and soon not at all. It was told to me that he did not want me to see him in this state. He worked odd jobs and lived from pillar to post and became homeless. He would come by to bathe and to get a hot meal. I was ten years old when the Great Depression of 1929 occurred, and I later heard it was during those cold winter months that my daddy's body was found frozen to death in a cold, lonely place. No one claimed his body, and there was a pauper's funeral since there was no money for a proper burial. No one in this great country should ever have to die alone. This hurts me until this very day.

"I began to have behavioral issues because somehow I felt I caused my mother and father's deaths. I was an angry, little boy, and with as much love as my aunt and uncle had doted on me, they still did not know how to deal with an angry boy. They tried tough love, but when I, in anger, slapped my little cousin, Mary, because she said something I didn't like, I was sent to live in a boys' home. My aunt cried a river of tears the day I left for that home. My uncle did not want to see me go, but I had gotten out of control, and they were at wits end as to what to do with me. My uncle was a strong man and could have easily broken every bone in my body, but for some reason, he didn't spank me. Maybe it was because he was my uncle by way of being married to my father's sister, and my aunt had forbid him to spank me. During this time, parents spanked their children as part of their disciplinary methods. And maybe, just maybe, if my aunt would have let him spank me, I would have been OK. Even Mary cried when I left for the boys' home. I did not cry. I was too angry to cry.

"When the car arrived to pick me up, one of the workers tried to take the suitcase my aunt packed full of clothes. I told him I could carry my own suitcase. I was seething with anger. I began the short walk to the door and to the waiting automobile outside that had a sign on the door that read, 'Happy Days Orphanage.' When I had reached the front porch, my uncle, who had been standing there, left the porch and did not tell me goodbye. My aunt, who had followed us outside, stooped down, while still crying, and kissed me on my cheek. She promised to come and see me as often as she could. The orphanage was only fifty miles away, but back in those days, fifty miles seemed like a long ways away.

"The orphanage was terrible. The staff brutally beat the children, and we were often neglected and suffered from physical and verbal abuse. There were rules, and the penalty for breaking rules would often be the absence of meals. The saddest of things was that we had been threatened and told when our family came to visit, we should not (and it was best for us) tell a soul what was really going on in that terrible place. We often wore long-sleeved shirts and clothing that hid the abuse from our family and visitors.

"True to her word, my aunt would come as often as she could, and Mary would always accompany her. When I saw Mary with her big, bright smile, I knew she had forgiven me. She ran up to me and gave me the tightest of hugs. That is when I began to cry. It was also on this visit that I asked my aunt if I could come back home. I was about to learn this one, hard truth, that once you become a ward of the state, getting back home was not that simple. The state and federal government were in charge of many of those orphanages, and money became the main factor and not the well-being of the kids. My uncle could never bring himself to come and see me in that place, so he never accompanied my aunt. I sort of knew in my heart if my uncle knew what was happening to me in that place, he would be found guilty of murder. He actually could kill a man with his bare hands.

"It would be two years later that I was allowed to leave the place that began to wear the name 'HELL' for us. It was only when two little boys were found dead that this orphanage was closed down, and I was allowed to go home. We never found out how these boys died because our mistreatment never happened in the view of other boys. Each of us knew because we heard the horrible screams of pain, the shrieks, and sounds of terror coming from the lashes with electrical cords and ropes, and we saw the cigarette burns on our skin. We saw nothing but heard everything, and what we heard and experienced kept us quiet. I knew it was because my aunt visited so often that I was protected from the worst of the abuse. I still show on my body some eighty plus years later the marks and reminders of my days in hell. Some of the other boys were not so lucky and suffered sexual abuse. If your family or loved ones put you in that orphanage and sort of just left you there, you suffered the greater abuse. Upon my release by the state and back into the custody of my aunt and uncle's care, I was able to tell my aunt and uncle the atrocities of that place. He was never the same.

"I saw the same disease that had killed my father take over his life. He could never forgive himself for sending me to that place. If the truth be told, I had forgiven him and my aunt the first time she had come to visit me and every time thereafter. I even told him, 'Dad, I forgive you.' I knew my uncle was not my real father because they reminded me many times of who my father was. They did not want me to be so sheltered from that truth that when I grew up and found out the truth, I would be totally devastated. So, in terms and language I could understand, they told me the truth of my real father from the beginning, but my uncle was the only dad I really knew. He was my dad in every way that counted most. He loved me, and I knew it. This strong man was never afraid or ashamed to say he loved me.

"This orphanage had taught us self-hatred by telling us that we were placed there because no one loved us, and if you received no visitors, it was a lot easier to believe those words. While I was told that the disease of alcoholism quickly killed my father, I watched it as it slowly began to kill my uncle. We tried to love the alcohol out of him. We tried to pray this disease out of him, and nothing at the time seemed to work. I loved him and did not want to see him die. I already had enough tragedy in my life and didn't want to see anymore. I would soon learn that my youth and life would be marred in tragedy.

While my uncle fought for his soul, one day I heard my aunt coughing a cough that never seemed to go away. It was a horrible-sounding cough. It was a cough that made it hard for her to go into the fields to work, but she did. At this time, she even worked harder trying to make up for the work my uncle had left undone because of his many drunken stupors while working in the fields. My aunt and uncle were some of the greatest sharecroppers Mr. Willis had. We children went to the school right up the road from Mr. Willis's fields. Unlike other families who made their children quit school, my aunt and uncle knew it was through education that we would make a better life for ourselves. They worked extra hard in those fields to send us to school. We only joined them on weekends and in the summertime.

"My aunt was still coughing nonstop when I passed by the slightly opened door of the bathroom. She had run to the bathroom from her room. Her coughing seemed to be getting worse, as she was telling all of us to stay away because she didn't want any of us to become sick. She did not know if what she had was contagious or not. I, too, rushed to the bathroom to see if I could help her. I then noticed that she had coughed up a bloody discharge into a white towel and was trying to hide the towel from our view. What did this mean? As a young adolescent, I really didn't know, but it just didn't feel right. I ran from the doorway, as if I had never seen anything at all, and she just went straight to the fields to work. It was a Saturday, so I went out to the fields to work as well. Mr. Willis had come to his fields that day to visit the workers, as he had done many times before. He was a good man to work for. He came to where we were working and heard that horrible cough that continued to plague my aunt. He did not like the way my aunt was coughing or breathing and told my father to take her home, and he would call the doctor to come by our house. I saw the worried look on my uncle's face and got that funny feeling all over again. I decided to stay in the fields and keep my cousins there. We all knew how to work in the fields.

"My uncle and aunt never returned to the fields that day, and I had to gather my cousins together for our ride in the wagon back to our home. We did not live far from the fields. My uncle was on the front porch with his face in his hands. Mr. Willis and the doctor were on the porch as well. I then saw the doctor shake Mr. Willis's hand and leave. Next, my strong uncle placed his head in the lap of Mr. Willis's shoulder and cried. I had seen my uncle cry before, but this sorrow was deep and had weighed heavy on him; so heavy that it buckled his knees. Mr. Willis had to try and hold him up. It was then that I jumped down from the wagon and ran up the porch to help Mr. Willis as he tried to hold up this strong man I had come to love. Mr. Willis and I were able to lower him down to a seated position on the porch as the tears poured from his eyes. It was as if the flood gates of sorrow had opened, and I had never seen so much grief.

"When my mother—my aunt—had gotten the news of my father, her brother, she cried a river. I had seen her grieve, but watching my uncle tore me up on the inside, and I groaned and began to cry. I hadn't noticed, but my cousins had jumped down from the wagon and had joined us on the porch. We had not only joined my uncle on the porch, we had also joined him in his tears. At this time, we did not even know why we were crying. We just knew it was really bad news. Mr. Willis hugged us all, and as he left, he told my uncle not to worry because he would take care of everything. What did that mean? Soon, my uncle paused between his tears to tell us that my aunt and their mother—my mother, too—had tuberculosis, known as TB. What was TB? He said it was a terrible disease, and the floodgates opened again. By the look on my cousins' faces, we all were wondering what that meant. We had many questions, so I prayed and asked God to help my uncle to stop crying and answer the many questions that clouded our minds. When he saw the look on our faces, his tears dried up long enough for him to explain.

"He explained that TB was a disease of the lungs, and it was highly contagious, and my aunt had contracted it from someone else. She would have to be placed in isolation and would therefore be kept away from us and all people, in fear of others contracting what she had. He told us the word was called 'quarantine.' We would also have to wait and see if we had been contaminated. He said we would all have to be examined by the doctor.

"That night, we all slept in the farthest room away from my aunt, and we opened all the windows. The next morning, Mr. Willis and a group of carpenters showed up at our house with lumber and screen in order to build a small air room in the yard away from the house. My uncle told us that fresh air was the best remedy for TB patients, but there was no real cure. All the bedding, mattresses, clothes, and linen in our house had to be burned because the doctor said they had been contaminated. We just could not take any chances because many people who contracted TB died.

"Neighbors brought us more clothes and linen. Mr. Willis saw to it that we had fresh mattresses for our beds. We scrubbed everything in the house, all while leaving the windows and doors open for a few days. We were not allowed to enter the air room where my aunt lived. We could only stand a distance and talk to her. Friends and neighbors were really kind to our family during this time. They all helped my uncle with my aunt, bringing soups and other healthy foods for healing.

"We all prayed hard daily, but it was not to be. Three weeks after the air room was built, my aunt died. One of the few people who had truly loved me for me was gone. For three weeks, we had to stay away from her. For three weeks, we could not hold her, and she couldn't hug us. For three weeks, there were no goodnight kisses. For three weeks, no touching at all, and then she died. I didn't know whether to feel sadder for my uncle or for me. He had not touched her in three weeks nor felt her touch, and now she was gone.

"We had to spread the news about her death. In those days, there were no good communication avenues. Everything was done mainly by word of mouth, especially if you were poor. My uncle gave us children little notes he wrote along with nails and a hammer, so we could go around town nailing her death announcement for all to see. This would allow the word to spread because those who read the signs could inform others.

"Female friends and neighbors came all bundled up, complete with gloves and masks to wash her body and get it ready for viewing. They had to protect themselves from contracting TB. Mr. Willis arrived with a wooden coffin in his wagon. After the body was cleaned and dressed, the women hung a white sheet on the wall to use as a backdrop. The coffin was placed in front of the sheet. We children were sent to neighbors to collect flowers from their gardens and from the side of the roads. We ran back to the air house holding some of the most beautiful flowers I had ever seen. Then the women pinned those fresh flowers to the white sheet, creating a wall of fragrant beauty. At this time, we were all finally allowed to visit my aunt's body. We all cried.

"That was the last day my uncle took a drink. He had promised his wife that he would sober up and take care of us. He didn't even drink socially anymore. My uncle never married again and spent the rest of his life making sure we finished high school and college. I became an engineer, and Mary became a doctor. Mary's younger sister became a nurse, and her brother became a science teacher. My uncle had done well, and after he quit drinking, he became a foreman over a group of men. Mr. Willis and his wife had no children, so they willed everything to my uncle when they died. Even though my uncle became rich, we children refused to take any money from him because we were pretty successful in our own right and wanted him to enjoy his own money and fortune. We all had gotten married and had plenty of children of our own, giving him plenty of grandchildren whom he doted over, every single one of them. Of course, all of his grandchildren doted over him, too.

"But all of the success in the world could not stop what happened next in my life, and I would give up all my riches if it could change what happened to us. After marrying, I moved my family to another state for a more prosperous life. There was a pond on our land that brought us much joy. We had taught our children how to swim, fish, and ice skate on this pond. In the summer, it was good for swimming and fishing, and in the winter, it was great for ice skating because it would freeze solid and thick. One winter day, it got quite warm, and I was bringing the children to skate on the pond because it was still frozen solid. My wife was going to join us later because she was preparing hot cocoa to bring out. The kitchen window overlooked the pond. As I headed out of the door with the kids, the telephone rang, and I told all the kids to wait and let me answer the phone. It was their grandfather calling to see how we were doing. My wife had been watching and had seen my son run toward the pond, rushing to put on his skates as I spoke with my father. The other children had stayed back with me, patiently waiting. My son began to skate on the icy pond. Suddenly, my wife yelled out a shrieking scream, a scream of horror, saying our oldest son, who was just ten, had fallen through the ice.

"I ran as fast as I could to the pond as my wife kept the other children away. I saw him under the ice as I tried to break through to get to where he was. I finally got to the spot he had fallen through, and I, too, was under ice. All of a sudden, he went deeper under the frigidly freezing water, and I could not see him. I went under the water, frantically searching for him. He knew how to swim, but the freezing water immobilized him. In the dark, murky water of the pond, I could only hope through touch that I could locate him. By this time, our good neighbor, Mr. Johnson, heard the curdling screams of my wife and had run to the pond with a hammer to join me. He began to break the ice, risking his own life, trying to rescue my son. He had managed to break through some of the icy pond, and we both went down again, searching for my son, our son. My father was still on the phone, for I had not hung up. He was yelling to my wife, asking what was happening, and my wife, in between crying and screaming, was keeping the other children inside. She told my father that Johnny had fallen into the icy pond, and she would have to hang up. She needed to dial zero for the operator. The operator would ask for an address so she could dispatch an ambulance. It's a good thing Mrs. Johnson had arrived and taken the phone so she could give the correct information of the emergency. My wife was too upset to give correct information. All of this took place before the advanced improvements of the automotive and quick response of 911. Mrs. Johnson helped to calm down my wife and children. Another neighbor, Mrs. Smith, also heard the commotion and had run toward the pond. She informed us that help was on the way. We were still diving under the icy water, trying to locate Johnny. Time seemed to move slowly in these moments. The pond that had seemed so small before now seemed like an ocean. I frantically searched with my hands to find my son, my firstborn son. I finally found what felt like a body. It was Johnny. I brought him up, and at the same time, Mr. Johnson had come up from his search. Mr. Smith, who was standing on the bank, quickly took Johnny from my arms and began to perform CPR. He had gained this knowledge as a medic in the army. The ambulance arrived, and the medics took over trying to resuscitate my son. I stood there praying, begging, asking God not to let my son die. I told God; I reminded God of all the tragedy I had seen in my life, and I just felt that God would not let my son die. We all prayed while the medics worked.

"They worked on my son but could not find a pulse. They placed him in the ambulance, and I got in, waving to my wife, who had finally been calmed down by Mrs. Johnson and Mrs. Smith. As we raced to the hospital, I never gave up hope. I continued to pray. They rushed him into the emergency room, and the doctors worked frantically on my son, my firstborn baby. I waited for what seemed to be an hour when one of the doctors came with the saddest news. 'We're sorry. We did all we could. Your son is dead.' No! This can't be. Not my son, not my firstborn son! Not the one that had carried my first and last name. No! God would not do this to me. Not to me, who had seen so much tragedy in my lifetime.

"God pulled me through the other tragedies before, but how can I make it through this one? How dare I go back home without Johnny? How do I walk through that door and tell my wife and four children that her son, their brother, will walk with us here no more? I couldn't bear the thought of seeing their reactions. Mr. Johnson had rushed into his house, changed out of his cold, wet clothes, and was now standing beside me as I got this terrible news. He had driven to the hospital to give me support. I was blessed with great neighbors. We had been there for each other through some of our saddest and happiest moments. There were weddings, births, funerals, storms, financial losses, birthdays; we shared many moments together, so it was no surprise to me that Mr. Johnson, my friend and neighbor, would be there for me. I was not even surprised that he dove into that frigidly freezing water. Mr. Johnson was one of the reasons I loved the great country called America. We take care of each other. We had stood in that emergency waiting room and cried together.

"As he drove me back home, a voice in my mind kept saying, 'This is your fault, your fault. You should have demanded that he wait for you when you saw him run to that pond. It's your fault. It's your fault.' The voice kept speaking these hurtful words, and I began to think that maybe the voice was right. When I approached the door, holding my key in my hand, I never noticed my wife had been looking out of the window between the curtains. Mrs. Johnson and Mr. and Mrs. Smith were there. When I walked in without Johnny by my side, everyone knew the terrible news. My friend, my best friend, my lover, my wife, my rock, the mother of my children, began to cry uncontrollably and repeated these words I can still hear until today: 'Not my baby, not my baby, not my baby!' She said these words over and over again. I went to her and put my arms around her to try in my feeble efforts to comfort her, but it didn't help. She cried a torrent of tears. My neighbors' wives were now crying on the shoulders of their husbands, and they, too, tried to bring them some type of comfort.

"Our other children had cried themselves to sleep, and we felt no real reason to awaken them with this sad news. We would do that in the morning. I was able to sit my wife down on our sofa as she was still crying. She had cried so much that she was exhausted and finally fell asleep in my arms while sitting on the sofa. She had literally cried for hours, and that is when my great neighbors decided to go home to get some rest for they, too, were exhausted. I told them I would wake my wife because she would want to thank them, but they motioned with their hands and whispers to let her sleep now. They said they would see us in the morning.

"It was as if they knew that in the next few months and years, sleep would evade us, and we would look for peaceful sleep and could not find her. I quietly carried my wife to our bedroom, careful not to wake her. I dared not try to remove her clothing to put on her sleeping attire in fear of waking her. This night's sleep, she needed. I carefully placed her in bed and covered her. Then I left the room for to check on the other kids who were in their bedrooms. They were still fast asleep. Did I mention we were blessed with five children, two boys and three girls? The girls shared a room, and the boys shared a room. I peeked in the girls' room first, and then I peeked in my boys' room. My youngest son was fast asleep and was a hard sleeper. He could sleep through an earthquake, and I was glad for this as I peeked through the door.

"An overwhelming sense of sadness swept over me. One of the beds in this room would not have its covers turned down. One of these beds would not give to its occupant a good night's sleep. So, I quietly slipped into the room, got into that bed, and cried. My son, my firstborn, was gone. Of course, the bed was too small for me, and my feet hung over the edge, but this bed was not made for me. It was his bed, the place he would run and cry when he was disappointed or could not get his way, the bed where he would place his baseball cards when he wanted to look at them. Some had been autographed by actual players. This bed brought him much comfort in his short time here. It was in this bed that I thought I heard a voice saying 'It is OK, Dad. I am all right. It was not your fault. I should have known better than to run to that pond without you.'

"I stopped my crying and swore I could hear an audible voice repeat those words. Then I knew we would be OK. I quietly got out of my son's bed as to not awake my other son and quietly closed the door behind me. As I walked toward our bedroom, I swore I heard that voice again. My wife was still fast asleep when I lay next to her and fell asleep from sheer emotional exhaustion.

"The next morning I felt the sun rays as they peeked through the curtains, and for a moment thought last night was just a terrible dream. So, upon waking, I found that bed empty. Still dazed, I ran to the kitchen. No sign of my son. My running from room to room had awakened the whole house, and now, here we all were in the kitchen. It was not a dream. My wife slowly walked to the kitchen window and looked out and began to sob quietly, much differently than the night before. My other four children asked as they wiped sleep from their eyes where Johnny was, why he had not slept in his bed, and was he still in the hospital? It was time. How do you talk to those so young about death? What do you say? What can you say? We all sat down at the kitchen table, and that woman who had been a sobering mass of mess and tears now found in herself the strength in her quiet way to talk to our children. Just a few hours ago, she had cried herself to the point of exhaustion. A few hours ago, she was not consolable, and now, how did she find the courage to be strong? It was as if she knew because I had been so strong for her that I needed her now.

"It was now my time to be the sobering mass of mess and tears, and for some reason, right there in front of our kids, I lost it. Soon I found myself on the floor in the fetal position, crying beyond control. This meltdown totally scared my children, but I couldn't stop. I begged God not to allow my children to see me like that. But God had not answered my other precious prayer and my firstborn son was gone. Why did he have to be taken away at that time? I actually began to believe that the culmination of all my previous tragedies had come flooding in at the wrong time. My wife, in her now quiet strength, had managed to get the children, who were frantically upset and crying, out of the kitchen. Mrs. Smith had arrived just in time to help move them to the dining room. And then that little woman got down on the floor and held me in her arms and didn't say a word. I just kept on crying, begging God again and again, and all of a sudden, I heard a child's voice say, 'It's OK, Daddy. I told you that I'm all right.' I looked around to see if any of our other children slipped from the watching eye of Mrs. Smith and saw no one. Then, in the depth of my being, I knew it was God sending his most recent angel to comfort my heart, and the tears dried up. I told my wife it was OK now. It really was OK. We both rose from the floor.

"It was time now. Mrs. Smith brought the children into the kitchen and quietly said that she would return later. Around that kitchen table, where I had said many prayers for our daily meals, around that table, where I had lead many discussions of proper behavior at home and at school, I didn't say a word. My wife spoke using words and language that children easily understood to tell them what had happened to their big brother. I could not have been more proud of this woman I had married. Our youngest child asked his mother if tonight, at prayer time, they could ask God to put an extra blanket on Johnny because he sometimes got cold at night. I finally spoke up and told him that we could.

"After our discussion, we were in no condition to cook, and no one seemed to want to eat, but our neighbors were already heading our way with breakfast they had prepared for us. We all nibbled on a little food, just enough for strength that we would need the next morning. My boss had already called and asked what he could do and to take as much time off as I needed.

"It was time for my wife and me to go to the morgue and begin the painful planning of a funeral. Mr. and Mrs. Smith had come over to watch the children. The ride to the morgue was quiet, but we did say enough to know what type of service we would conduct for our son. It would not be a funeral but a celebration. We wanted to celebrate the joy he had brought to us and others. It's not the quantity of life but the quality. As we viewed the body and held each other close, there seemed to be a smile on his face. Maybe it was because he always loved to see us hug.

"From the morgue, we called the funeral director. The celebration director, as we began to call him, asked us what we would like to have done. We told him a celebration. Our minister had met us there, and he, too, had heard we wanted a celebration. Instead of flowers, there would be toys, lot of toys. Johnny never really liked flowers, and afterward, we could donate the toys to an orphanage in his name. These toys would bring much joy to other kids. My wife had some unusual requests, it seemed, but the celebration director was great. She wanted to clean the body for the embalming process. She even wanted to pick out the suit he would wear; really, he only had one—he hated wearing suits. The celebration director accommodated us in every way he could.

"On the day of the funeral, there were toys and kids everywhere. I did not realize that Johnny had so many friends and had touched so many lives. His fifth-grade teacher, whom we knew he had a crush on, told of a flower he had brought to class, even at the ridicule of his classmates. As one little boy passed by the casket during the viewing, he placed a small, red car inside. This was the same car I had given him for his birthday. The little boy said, 'Thank you for the car you gave me when you found out my parents were too poor to give me a present for my birthday. My dad has a better job now, and I should have given this toy back to you before today.' A little girl had written a note that read 'Dear Johnny, my mother told me you were in heaven with God. Would you watch out for my little sister? She is up there, too.' I, too, had written a note that simply said, 'Thanks for the best ten years of my life—Dad.' I placed the note in his hand. I knew when he got the time, he would read it because he had a love for reading.

"There were tears, and tears are OK, but for the most part, there were smiles and laughter. Even his little sister asked to speak, and she said, 'I forgot to thank you for beating up Jimmy that day when he hit me while we were playing in the backyard.' I had wondered why Jimmy went home crying that day.

"I did realize that there would be days of crying left for us, even months and years. But today, I thanked God for the memories. For the next ten years, without my wife knowing, I would sneak off to the cemetery on his birthday and talk to the spot we had buried him. Of course, there were times we went as a family to place flowers on his grave, but no one knew of our secret meetings. I had been in secret grief. On that ten-year anniversary birthday, I heard a voice say, 'I am not here; live among the living.' And that was the last day of my secret 'me.' He had just told me life goes on, so live your life.

"I, we, began to live again. We had thought it was in sadness we remember our loved ones gone before, but it is in our living that we truly honor their existence. The truth is when life knocks you down, you get up and go on."

And as suddenly as Mr. Jolly had begun to share, he stopped, and the mood changed to a happy one. He continued.

"My life was filled with even more tragedy after my son's death, but understand this one thing, my friends, when life gives you lemons, you just make you know what. Lemon pie! And remember, life definitely *is* what you make it. The only thing left for me to say is this. I am still happily married to that woman, my wife, my lover, my best friend. We have five children, twenty grandchildren, thirty-one great grandchildren, and nine great-great grandchildren." Then he smiles and says, "My wife is pregnant again!" We all said, "OK, Mr. Jolly, you are pushing it now!"

Chapter Seven

THEY'RE EVERYWHERE

If you ever slow down long enough, if you ever decide to walk through life and not run, if you would only pause a bit, if you ever decide not to hurry to your destination and just enjoy the scenery and the journey, you just *might* see them. You just *might* notice them. They are everywhere, in every place. They are all around us. They are not invisible.

Their skin may not be clear anymore and may be full of age spots. Their skin may also be folded with deep lines and wrinkles. The sweet noise of sound sometimes escapes them. Their hair is of a different color from youth. Their strength may be weakening. Their eyes have dimmed, but they have seen more than we have seen. Their steps have shortened, but they still continue to move forward. Ask them about an hour ago, and they may become disoriented. But ask them about time past, and they remember stories in vivid details and become alive again, for they love telling those old stories.

They still drive. They still drink alcoholic beverages. They still even make love and are in love. They are still alive and energetic. They are still health conscious and physically active. They are still curious about life and willing to learn new things. They are still politically active and have great ideas about how government should effectively run. They still cry at good movies and laugh at funny jokes. They remind us of what is most important, and they teach us not to dwell on insignificant non-sense. And if we have listened, they have shown us how to handle life's successes and failures with pride and dignity. They are the human race's greatest teachers.

Old people have built up influence. They possess a confidence from having already gone through paths we are headed. They don't have to tell us how; they have shown us how. All of them have a story. Listen to their defining moments in life, and you just might learn something.

Have you ever noticed how calm old folks are? This is not due to being ignorant of events going on around them. This is due to a confidence of knowing that they *know* what they know. Old folks have learned that the world keeps spinning on its axis, no matter what. While younger folks are hustling and scrambling like ants, these old folk just cruise along through life and enjoy the scenery. They handle life in bite-size chunks.

Sometimes we ignore them. Sometimes we think they are not important. Sometimes we think they are in the way and treat them as if they are a nuisance. Sometimes we think they don't know anything. Sometimes we think they are not aware of anything. Sometimes we think they actually live in a fog, ignorant of what's going on right in front of them.

They are not aliens; they are real flesh and blood, skin and bones. They still have thoughts and dreams, hopes and fears. They are a part of us; they *are* us. They have been where we are, and soon, we will go where they have been. They are old folks, and watch out! They are coming out to *play*.

www.ingramcontent.com/pod-product-compliance
Lightning Source LLC
Chambersburg PA
CBHW051300170626
46809CB00004B/1735